mary-kateandashley

Sweet 16

D1363020

mary-kateandashley

Sweet 16
WISHES AND DREAMS

Kathy Clark

HarperCollins*Entertainment*
An Imprint of HarperCollins*Publishers*

A PARACHUTE PRESS BOOK

A PARACHUTE PRESS BOOK
Parachute Publishing, LLC
156 Fifth Avenue
Suite 325
NEW YORK
NY 10010

First published in the USA by HarperEntertainment 2002
First published in Great Britain by HarperCollins*Entertainment* 2002
HarperCollins*Entertainment* is an imprint of HarperCollins*Publishers* Ltd,
77-85 Fulham Palace Road, Hammersmith, London W6 8JB

SWEET 16 books are created and produced by Parachute Press, LLC, in
cooperation with Dualstar Publications, a division of Dualstar Entertainment Group,
LLC, published by HarperEntertainment, an imprint of HarperCollins Publishers.

The HarperCollins website address is
www.**fire**and**water**.com

1 3 5 7 9 8 6 4 2

The author asserts the moral right to be
identified as the author of the work.

ISBN 0 00 714880 1

Printed and bound in Great Britain by Clays Ltd, St Ives plc

chapter one

"Calm down, Mary-Kate." I opened my purple notebook to my "Sweet Sixteen Party – To-Do" list. "Here's what we have to do. If we just follow this list, everything will be all right."

Together we read the list.

(1) Go to post office – get invitations back.

(2) Call Wilson!

(3) Redo the guest list to include boys.

(4) Mail out new invitations.

Mary-Kate pointed to the first item on the list. "See, we already have a problem," she complained. "How are we going to get the invitations back? They're sitting in the post office right now!

"The city bus lurched to a stop at a red light. It was Friday afternoon, and Mary-Kate and I were rushing to the post office.

Our party planner, Wilson Miller, mailed our

party invitations that afternoon. Wilson was planning our sweet sixteen as a favour to Dad. You would think that throwing a party would be easy with the help of a professional planner. But somehow Mary-Kate and I made it very complicated.

At first we wanted to have an all-girl sweet sixteen – so we invited fifty girls. The invitations addressed to those fifty girls were sitting in the post office, ready to be delivered.

But then Mary-Kate and I changed our minds. She wanted to invite her boyfriend, Jake Impenna – and I wanted to invite my new boyfriend, Ben. How could we celebrate our sweet sixteen without them? So we wanted to uninvite half the girls and invite twenty-five boys.

The problem was, we didn't tell Wilson in time. And once the girls received their invitations, there would be no way we could uninvite them. That would be mortifying!

The bus stopped in front of the post office. Mary-Kate looked determined. "Operation Rescue-the-Invites begins," she announced.

"Next?" a mail clerk behind the counter called.

Ashley and I sprinted up to the counter. As we approached the clerk, I noticed that she was wearing a yellow smiley-face button on her cardigan sweater. She had another pin next to it that said SERVICE WITH A SMILE – GUARANTEED. I hoped she was as friendly and cheerful as her sweater said she was.

"May I help you?" the clerk asked.

"Yes, thank you – Nancy," I said, sneaking a peek at her name tag. "We have a problem. We're having a sweet sixteen party in a few weeks, and someone just dropped off the invitations here – to be mailed. But there's a *huge* mistake on them, so we've got to get them back."

"Hey! I think I see the invitations right over there!" Ashley pointed to a white box sitting on a metal cart behind the clerks' stations. "Those square envelopes that look like CD covers – that's them!"

I squinted at the cart and gasped. "That *is* them! Could we have them back, please?"

"Hold on, girls. We're not even sure those are the correct items," Nancy said. "And even if they were, I'm not allowed to—"

"Look!" Ashley grabbed my sleeve. "That's Wilson's logo on the side of the box. Those are *definitely* our invitations."

"Excellent! We can just take them back before anyone sees them," I said.

I smiled. This was all working out so easily!

Nancy shook her head. "No, girls, I'm afraid I can't help you. We're not allowed to return mail once it's been given to us."

"*What?*" I slumped against the counter.

I couldn't believe that Nancy wouldn't help us. Maybe I should tell her the whole story.

"My boyfriend broke up with me because of this mix-up. . . ." I said. I felt tears prickling the backs of my eyelids. "I told Jake the party was for girls only – but then Ashley invited her boyfriend, Ben, and Jake heard about it. Jake thought I lied to him! And now he isn't speaking to me!"

Nancy reached over and patted my arm. "That's terrible! You poor thing. My daughter went through a terrible break-up last month, too."

"So . . . you understand?" I looked at her and blinked away a tear. "You'll make an exception and give those envelopes back to us?"

"What? Oh, no." Nancy shook her head. "I'm sorry, girls, but there's nothing I can do."

I watched as one of the postal workers approached the metal cart. He pushed it around the counter and out into the hallway. I gulped. In a second, our invitations would be in a truck and on their way to fifty girls!

"Please," I begged. "My relationship is at stake here!"

"Not to mention our social lives!" Ashley added. "We will *not* be popular if we have to uninvite twenty-five girls from our party!"

"No one will ever talk to us again," I said. I leaned on the counter, did an extreme slump and tried to look as pathetic as I could. "We'll be complete outcasts." I paused. "Let's face it, Ashley. Our social life is now officially over."

Nancy's expression didn't change. She looked over our heads to the line that had formed behind us. "Next!" she called.

We shuffled down the counter, away from Nancy's window. I glanced over at the metal cart, where our invitations still sat. The postal worker had stopped in the hallway. The cart itself was within easy reach.

"Wait a second!" I whispered to Ashley. "We're not going anywhere yet. I have a plan."

"What is it?" Ashley asked in a soft voice.

"We have to cause a distraction," I whispered.

"Why?" Ashley wanted to know.

"Just do it!" I said.

Ashley walked towards the exit and then pitched forward to the floor, throwing her arms into the air with dramatic flair. "Yikes!" she cried as she tumbled forward on to the slick linoleum floor.

"Perfect," I said under my breath.

"Oh, dear. Are you all right?" the worker pushing the cart asked. He rushed over to check on Ashley, leaving the cart completely and totally unguarded.

Two more people – including Nancy – followed right behind.

"Don't move, Ashley!" I cried. "I'll call a doctor."

Ashley had just enough time to glance up at me with a confused look before the entire staff of clerks and customers crowded around her. "Honey, let me have a look at that ankle," Nancy said.

I ran towards the hallway where our invitations were abandoned. Excellent! No one had seen me. I tiptoed over to the metal cart. I grabbed the box of invitations.

I checked the return address on the envelopes to make sure I had the right box. Yes! They *were* our invitations! Now all I had to do was get them out of the post office!

With the box under my arm, I sneaked towards the front door.

"What do you think you're doing?" a man's deep voice bellowed.

I looked up, and came face to face with a stern-looking man in a brown suit.

"Exactly where do you think you're going with that box, young lady?" the man asked.

"Um . . . isn't this the mail drop?" I asked.

chapter two

"Look on the bright side, Mary-Kate. We may not have got the invitations back, but at least the postmaster didn't call our parents."

My sister and I were lying on my bed, trying not to get too upset about the invitation fiasco.

"I mean, who would have thought that taking mail back from the post office is a federal offence?" I asked.

"Whoop-de-doo," Mary-Kate mumbled. She was lying on her stomach with her face pressed into the duvet. I could barely hear her muffled voice. "I'm so thrilled."

"Hey, we're lucky they let us go," I reminded her.

Mary-Kate turned over on to her back. "Yeah. Lucky. I just feel so *lucky* right now," she said.

I whomped her with one of my pillows.

I knew she was upset about Jake – and I

totally understood. Mary-Kate was crazy about him, and he wouldn't talk to her! But I wasn't going to let her wallow in misery.

I moved over to my desk and flipped on my computer. I signed on to my e-mail account. "Plan A failed. So *now* we come up with Plan B."

Mary-Kate stared at the ceiling. She tossed a pillow up and down, thinking. "Maybe there's some way we can stop all the invitations from being put in people's mailboxes," she suggested.

"Could we slip the mailed invites out of everyone's mailboxes before they read them?" I asked.

Mary-Kate cleared her throat. "Ashley, I know you're organised and all. But I don't see how we can be *fifty* places at once when the mail is delivered."

"Okay, bad idea," I laughed. "Forget that."

I opened up a 'send mail' window on my computer. "I'm going to e-mail Brittany and Lauren," I said. "Maybe they can help us."

"Good idea," Mary-Kate said.

Brittany and Lauren were our best friends. They had the best ideas for salvaging any bad situation. We knew we could count on them to help us.

I had just entered Brittany's e-mail address, when an Instant Message flashed on the right side of my screen. It was from Ben! A smile spread across my face as I read:

Hey, Ashley – I saw that you were online so I

wanted to ask – how about going to the Eastside mall with me on Monday after the drivers' ed class?

"Who's it from?" Mary-Kate asked as she sat up on the bed.

"Ben," I told her excitedly.

Mary-Kate climbed off the bed. She grabbed my extra chair to sit beside me at the desk. "What did he say?"

"He wants me to go to the mall," I told her.

"So are you going?" Mary-Kate asked.

"Of course!" I said. I typed in my answer. Ben and I went to different schools, so for a boyfriend and girlfriend we didn't see each other often – except in drivers' ed on Mondays and Wednesdays.

I glanced at my calendar: I had only four more lessons of so-called behind-the-wheel instruction before our drivers' tests.

Mary-Kate sighed. "I wish Jake would ask me to meet *him* at the mall. Of course, he'd have to stop being mad at me before that would ever happen."

"Don't worry – you guys will get back together," I said.

"How can you be so sure?" Mary-Kate asked. "I'm not." She picked up the Magic 8-ball on my desk. "Will Jake and I get back together?" She swirled the ball around and looked at the cube floating inside for an answer.

"Reply hazy – try again later?" Mary-Kate groaned. "That's not what I wanted to see."

"You can't go by *that*," I said. Another IM blinked on to my screen. Ben again. *Okay – talk to you tonight*. We IM'd each other goodbye. Then I wrote to Brittany and Lauren, begging for our best friends' help.

After we sent the message, Mary-Kate leaned back in her chair. "Okay, so what else can we do?"

"Hold on, let me check." I grabbed my purple notebook and scanned the list I'd written on the bus. "We've got to call Wilson," I said.

"Of course!" Mary-Kate said.

I looked for his phone number in my address book. "Where do you think he'll be this time?" I asked.

Wilson, our party planner, has a totally cool life. We met him because of our dad, who's in the music business.

Wilson is a major jet-setter type. He plans parties for celebrities and travels all over the world to do it. But he never stays in one place long. He could be in his L.A. home office one day, skiing in the Alps the next, and backstage at a concert in New York City after that! We can usually reach him on his mobile, but we never know where it's going to ring!

Mary-Kate ran downstairs to grab another phone, so we could be on the line at the same time. Wilson's number rang four times. I had almost given up hope, when there was a click. "This is Wilson."

"Hey, Wilson!" I said. "This is Ashley."

"And this is Mary-Kate. Wilson, we have a complete disaster on our hands!" she said.

"What? Hold on a second; let me find a quiet place where I can talk," Wilson said. In the background, I could hear loud music playing, and then people shouting to each other and applause. Then there was a click, as if Wilson had gone into a separate area and closed a door. "Now. What did you say about a disaster? Tell me the problem and I'll help."

"Okay, great." Mary-Kate quickly told Wilson about us changing our minds *after* he sent out fifty invitations. "So we either have to uninvite twenty-five girls – which we don't want to do, because that's rude and everyone will hate us. Or we have to invite fifty guys now, in order to have an equal number of girls and guys. That means we'll have to have one hundred guests, which is one *insanely huge* party!"

"Well, you're right, you can't *un*invite people," Wilson said. "So if you want to add guys, we have two problems. First, we need to clear this with your mom and dad. Second, we'll need to find a new place for the party."

"And we need to let everyone know that the

invitation they're about to get is totally *wrong*," I pointed out. "But how do we do that?"

"Hmm. Hold on a sec." Wilson was humming and tapping something against his phone. He didn't say anything for a minute, and I started to worry.

In the meantime, an IM from Brittany popped up on my computer screen.

That's when it hit me – the perfect solution!

"I know!" I yelled. "I've got it!"

Wilson laughed. "That was totally loud, so this better be good," he teased.

"It is," I said. "We can use e-mail! We can send an e-mail to all the people on our list – telling them that the invitation they're about to get in the mail doesn't tell the whole story – that there's new information!"

"Hey! That's perfect," Mary-Kate said. "We can tell them something like . . . our party has just become new and improved! Maybe that's what we can call it – Mary-Kate and Ashley's New and Improved Sweet Sixteen!"

Wilson laughed. "Excellent! An e-mail will create tons of buzz about your party. I don't even know why you guys called me – you've got this all figured out on your own."

"Not exactly!" I objected. "I mean, what do we *write* in this e-mail, since we don't know where the party is or *anything*?"

"Well, we can keep it vague for a while yet,"

12

Wilson said. "We've got a month until the party. So why don't you hint that people will have to stay tuned for the latest updates – that they'll need to check their e-mail daily for news on the big event. That'll build lots of hype."

"Okay, that sounds good," I agreed.

"And I'll start thinking of places we can have this new, bigger party," Wilson continued. "If we can stall people for a little while, that'll give us time to find a new location."

"Okay. When you say bigger . . . how much bigger?" I asked. I was worried about whether Mom and Dad would go for this!

"Well, it's like Mary-Kate said. Since you already invited fifty girls – and you can't take those invitations back – you should probably think about inviting fifty guys," Wilson said.

"Which means we have to ask Mom and Dad if we can have a hundred guests instead of fifty," Mary-Kate added. She looked at me and grimaced. Suddenly this didn't sound so easy any more.

"Guys, you're going to have to act fast. I'll work up a list of new locations – you talk to your parents, okay? As soon as possible." He covered the phone briefly and yelled, "Be right there." Then he came back on the line. "I hate to run, girls, but I'm in charge of a backstage party that starts in five minutes," Wilson said. "So – you'll talk to your parents about this tonight and don't send out the e-mail until we talk again – I'll be in the office in a few days and we'll meet then, okay?"

Mary-Kate and I said goodbye, then hung up our phones.

I looked at Mary-Kate. "So. Are you going to ask Mom if we can add fifty guests and have the party somewhere else, or am I?"

"We'll both do it. At dinner tonight," Mary-Kate said.

"Are you sure *you* don't want to do the talking?" I asked with a pleading look.

"All right, I'll do it," Mary-Kate said. "But you owe me."

"Deal," I agreed.

"And how was your day, Mom?" I smiled brightly at her as I stirred my bowl of pasta that night at dinner. "Everything okay at work today?"

Mom works at the Sunshine Day Care Centre. All the little kids there totally love her.

"I had a great day," she said. "Everything went exactly the way it was supposed to. Thanks for asking!"

"Oh, no problem," I said. "Boy, this pasta is good. It's *amazing*, actually."

"Thank you, Mary-Kate, but it's just my regular recipe. You must be hungry." Mom laughed. "So, what did you girls do after school today?"

Not much, I thought. *Just nearly got arrested for stealing some mail*. I smiled nervously. "Oh, nothing interesting," I said. "Very ordinary stuff. Homework. You know."

Under the table, Ashley nudged my foot with hers. I knew she wanted me to ask Mom about the new party plan, but I couldn't – not yet. I was working my way up to it.

"So I was thinking about your girl power theme this afternoon, after work," Mom announced. "I did some surfing online for decorating ideas. I want this place to look *really* cool for your party."

I gulped. We had to tell Mom we couldn't have the party here – and she was looking forward to it so much.

"So what did you come up with?" Dad asked as he passed the basket of garlic bread to Mom.

"Well, we can have Wilson get some stand-up cutouts of female superheroes," Mom said. "Like Wonder Woman, Super Girl. Maybe we could place them at the entrance to different rooms. I don't want the cartoon thing to seem young, though – so we'll contrast with photos of famous women – music celebrities, actresses, writers, politicians – a giant collage, maybe." She passed the bread to Ashley and smiled.

"Umm . . . great," Ashley mumbled. She set

down the basket without taking a piece of garlic bread.

"There's just so much to do. It's got to look perfect. We'll have to clear out some furniture to make room for dancing and mingling," she went on. "Right?"

"Of course," I murmured.

Ashley nudged me under the table again. I looked at her and shrugged. Mom seemed so happy. What was I supposed to do – tell her to just forget about her plans?

"What do you girls say?" Dad asked. "Mom's ideas sound good to me." He glanced from me to Ashley and back again.

"Yeah, they're, um, great," I said. *Do it, Mary-Kate! I told myself. Just tell them – you goofed and now you need to invite a hundred people to the party!* But I couldn't. I had to change the subject – and fast.

"So, speaking of our birthday. Is it time for us to begin the yearly present hunt?" I asked, stalling for time.

Every year since we were little, we've had this game with our parents. They always hide our birthday presents, and we always try to find them. "I was thinking you got us something like electronic organisers for our birthday. We'd probably never be able to find those, they're so small."

My mother shook her head. "Nope."

"Okay . . . let's see. How about clothes? Always possible. Or a trip somewhere? Wait – I know. New mountain bikes! Those are pretty hard to hide, though." I looked at Dad. "Well? No hints at all?"

He shrugged and took a sip of water. His face started to turn red. "We don't have any hints, because, uh, we didn't buy you guys a present this year."

I started laughing. Dad is the world's worst liar – he always blushes when he tries to, and he can barely get the words out without stammering a little. "Oh, sure, Dad," I teased him. "Right."

"What? I'm . . . I'm serious," he said, his face getting even redder.

"I know!" Ashley snapped her fingers. "You probably got us tickets to your music festival."

Dad shook his head. "Oh, no. No. Nope."

"Actually, Dad and I thought the sweet sixteen party would be your gift this year," Mom said, coming to his rescue.

I glanced at Ashley. We cared about the party a hundred times more than any present. And Mom and Dad were being so generous with us about it. How could we ask them to do anything more?

But we had to find a new place to hold the party right away – or there wouldn't be a party at all!

I could read the panic in Ashley's eyes. She had the same question burning in her mind – *What are we going to do?*

chapter three

"You know what I think?" I asked.

"That I look awful in green?" Mary-Kate turned around in front of the three-way mirror to check the fit of the shiny green strapless dress she had tried on. "Because this colour is terrible on me. Totally."

"Actually, I was thinking that I look like a football player." I frowned at the short puffy sleeves of the blue dress I had tried on.

"You do not," Mary-Kate said. "A hockey player, maybe."

We both laughed, and each grabbed another dress to try on from the rack outside the dressing room. "Finding the perfect party dress – take six!"

I said as we ducked into our separate room to change.

We were with Mom on Saturday at a cool boutique called Kick, shopping for our sweet sixteen dresses. So far we'd tried on five apiece, and hadn't liked any of them. I stepped back and looked at the pale yellow sleeveless linen dress I had tried on. It wasn't me, and it definitely wasn't Mary-Kate.

I walked out of the dressing room just as Mary-Kate came out in a sparkling black dress. "I think this would be good – *if* we were ten years older," Mary-Kate said, turning in front of the mirror.

"Same with this one," I said. "Golf, anyone?"

Mom came over to us, carrying two identical dresses. "Hey, look what I found. This is perfect," she said. She showed us a royal blue backless dress with a halter neck and a long, flowing blue skirt. The fabric was silk, and patterned with tiny white stars. "Any interest at all?"

"I don't know. It's kind of long, isn't it?" Mary-Kate asked. She glanced at me.

"It's pretty, though," I said as Mom handed one of the dresses to me. The tiny white stars on the dress sparkled in the light.

"I brought one for each of you, so you could try them on at the same time," Mom said. "I really think this dress would be so beautiful on both of you."

"I don't know . . ." Mary-Kate frowned and held the dress up against her.

"Just try it!" Mom laughed. She gently pushed Mary-Kate towards her dressing room door.

"Okay, okay," Mary-Kate said.

I closed my dressing-room door and changed

out of the yellow dress. Then I took the dark-blue one off its hanger. As soon as I slipped it over my shoulders and fastened the halter tie behind my neck, I knew it was the dress for me. I gazed at my reflection in the narrow full-length mirror. I could just imagine Mary-Kate and me making a grand entrance at the party in these dresses. And then I'd be dancing with Ben. . . .

With every step I took, the silk fabric flowed around my body. I felt totally glamorous – like a movie star walking onstage to accept an Oscar.

"Wow!" Mom said as I came out of the dressing room. "You look gorgeous." Mary-Kate walked out a second later and twirled around. "You look gorgeous, too!" Mom said.

Mary-Kate and I looked at each other. "Well?" I asked excitedly. "What do you think?"

"I can't believe it. This dress is amazing!" Mary-Kate said. "I definitely love it. How about you?"

"I love it, too," I said.

"That could be a problem," Mom worried.

"Maybe not," I said. "I mean . . . we haven't done this in a really, really long time. And you might think it's silly and babyish . . . but I think we should both wear this dress to the party."

"You do, Ashley?" Mom asked.

I nodded. "It makes sense for our sweet sixteen. Because if we wear the same dress, neither one of us will look more important or more special or—"

"More anything than the other?" Mary-Kate finished.

"Yeah. We'll just be who we are, which happens to be nearly identical – and it'll sort of call attention to our bond as sisters. Not to mention that these dresses look really cool. But if you hate the idea, then forget I ever mentioned it."

Mary-Kate grinned. "I think it's a great idea. And it's going to make it way easier for us to pick out our jewellery and shoes, because we can just get two of everything."

Mom dabbed at her eyes with a tissue. "I think it's a very sweet idea. And I don't think you'll regret it for one second." She gave a little sniffle. "I can't wait to see you walk into your party in those!"

Mom pulled the back of my dress a little tighter. "You might need a few little alterations to make these fit perfectly – I'll get the saleswoman. But you know, once the alterations are done . . . and all the *house* alterations are done . . . this is going to be one amazing night."

I glanced at Mary-Kate, feeling a little uneasy. We still needed to ask Mom if we could add fifty guests to our party – *and* find a new place to have it!

"We have to tell her," I said.

"Okay, but you go first this time," Mary-Kate said.

"What do you mean, *this* time?" I said. "You never said anything to her last night at dinner."

"Oh. Well, you go first anyway," Mary-Kate insisted.

"No way! *You* go first," I said.

"Girls! I'm right here," Mom interrupted. "What do you need to say to me?"

I smiled nervously. "Can we wait until we get home so we can talk about it with Dad, too?"

Maybe, if I stalled a little longer, I could think of a better way to explain the reason we'd goofed.

"So what we'd like to do, if it's okay with you guys, is invite an equal number of boys to our party," I explained to Mom and Dad on Saturday afternoon. "But we already invited fifty girls, so that would mean we'd have a hundred guests. Which I know is a really big number—"

"A *hundred* guests?" Dad's eyes widened. "Are you serious?"

"Yes," Mary-Kate admitted. "We're sorry – we messed up because we got our signals crossed. And the thing is that we already invited fifty girls, so we have to stick to that."

Mom nodded. "Yes, you do. And if you want an equal number of boys . . . Well, what do you think?" she asked Dad.

He didn't say anything for a minute, and I held my breath.

"I guess it's all right with me," he finally

agreed. "But doesn't that mean we need to have the party somewhere else?"

"Yes, I think so," Mom said. "Because the idea of a hundred sixteen-year-olds in this house is a little much."

"I know. We're really sorry, Mom," Mary-Kate said. "We didn't mean to make you do all that work for nothing."

Mom waved this away. "I didn't do that much – don't worry about it."

"I'm sure Wilson can help you locate another venue," Dad said. "There is one thing to keep in mind, though."

"What's that?" Mary-Kate asked.

"Well, the party was originally planned for fifty guests," Dad began. "And you can invite as many boys as you like. But you'll have to stick to the original budget we made. That won't be easy if you have twice as many guests as you'd planned for."

I got a sinking feeling, but Mary-Kate took the news in her stride. "No problem," she said. "We can do it. Right, Ashley?"

"Sure," I agreed, trying to think of ways we could cut corners to make our money stretch. "It won't be easy, but—"

"Wilson's an expert on this," Dad said. "You three will have to work together to figure this out."

Mary-Kate nodded. "Okay. Sounds like a plan."

"Good." Dad looked pleased. "By the way, girls, I've been meaning to ask you . . . how are your driving lessons going?"

"Great!" Mary-Kate replied. "Our classroom work is done. We only have three more driving lessons before the big test, but I'm not worried. I *love* driving."

Three more lessons, I thought. Mary-Kate sounded so ready. *Why do I feel like I need* thirty *more lessons?*

"My two little girls – driving!" Mom sighed. "I can't believe it."

"Better get used to it, Mom," Mary-Kate joked. "I'm going to be entering NASCAR races soon."

Mom rolled her eyes, laughed, and turned to me. "How about you? Do you love driving, too?"

"Not exactly. But I definitely like it," I said. I thought about a couple of the disastrous things that had happened during my lessons. First I'd pulled on to the wrong side of the street. Then I'd knocked over Ben's mailbox. The lessons had gone better since then, but I still didn't feel confident about passing the test.

"So you'll both be ready for your driving tests?" Dad asked.

Mary-Kate nodded. "I can't *wait* to get my licence. There's just one thing I'm worried about, though."

"What's that?" Mom asked, concerned.

"That my licence photo will come out as badly as Dad's did," Mary-Kate teased.

Mom and Dad started laughing. I laughed, too, but I was thinking, *Is that really all she's worried about – a bad I.D. photo? Because what I'm worried about is passing the test!*

I tossed and turned in bed that night, visions of our sweet sixteen flashing before my eyes. Ashley and I appeared in our beautiful dresses, floating down a long staircase. Ben stood at the foot of the stairs and reached for Ashley's hand. I reached out my hand, but no one was there to take it. Ben and Ashley danced away, leaving me standing there alone.

I flicked on my nightstand light. Sometimes I felt a little restless on Sunday nights, but this was ridiculous. I'd been lying in bed for an hour and I hadn't even closed my eyes yet.

I couldn't stop thinking about Jake. I knew I'd see him the next day at school, and I was dying to talk to him – if only he'd let me! I really missed him. I knew he was hurt, and I felt terrible about it. But if he'd only let me explain, he wouldn't be hurt any more!

I flopped back against my pillow, groaning with frustration.

Maybe I shouldn't wait until school tomorrow,

I suddenly thought. What if I wrote him an e-mail *now*? That would be a lot less nerve-racking than trying to talk to him.

I got out of bed and turned on my computer. I pulled my robe around my shoulders and started to type:

Dear Jake—

Please don't delete this!

I know you're really angry and hurt because you think I don't want you at our party – but you're so wrong!   I want you there more than anyone else. It was just a big misunderstanding between Ashley and me.

I told you that we'd decided not to invite any guys because I thought that was what she wanted. I didn't know that at the very same time she'd changed   her mind and invited Ben.

My shoulders slumped as I reread what I'd written. I could just see Jake signing on to his e-mail, seeing a message from me, and hitting the Delete key.

Who was I kidding? An e-mail wasn't going to make it up to Jake. I needed to see him in person, meet him face to face.

I'll find Jake at school tomorrow, I told myself. *And no matter what, we're going to talk!*

chapter four

"Okay, Mary-Kate. Let's start with the facts. Your party is two weeks from Thursday and you don't know where you're having it yet?" Brittany raised her perfectly shaped eyebrows.

It was Monday afternoon, and school was over for the day. Brittany and I settled on a picnic table outside. She's African-American, with dark brown eyes, tight, short curls, and a no-nonsense attitude.

"At least it's okay with Mom and Dad," I told her. "Wilson's giving us a list of party places tomorrow." I tapped my feet nervously against the bench. A bunch of boys were playing basketball on a court nearby. One of them was Jake.

As soon as the game's over, I'm going to talk to him, I told myself. But every time I even *thought* about talking to him, I got so nervous my palms started sweating.

"Well," Brittany said. "You better hope this Wilson guy comes up with something good." She zipped up her orange hooded sweater.

"He will," I said. "I just hope the best places aren't already booked." I watched Jake dribble the ball towards the basket. He looked totally cute, wearing a black T-shirt, faded jeans and sneakers.

If we could just spend five minutes together, I knew I could clear up this whole misunderstanding. "Five minutes – is that so much to ask?" I muttered out loud.

"Five minutes for what?" Brittany looked puzzled.

"Sorry," I said. "Just thinking about talking to Jake."

"You're losing it, Mary-Kate," Brittany teased me. "Don't worry – you'll get to talk to him."

"I know – I'm just nervous."

Jake made a perfect lay-up. There was a loud cheer. The game was over. The guys picked up their jackets and backpacks and headed off in different directions.

"Here goes nothing," I told Brittany as I hopped off the picnic table.

"Good luck!" Brittany said.

I walked over to Jake, who was busily repacking something in his backpack. My stomach was doing flips. "Hey, Jake," I called, trying to sound casual. "Good game – that last lay-up was great!"

He stood and stared at me. His grey eyes didn't light up at all, the way they did before all this happened. "Thanks," he said.

"Um-um – I was wondering if you wanted to do something. Together," I stammered. "Like grab a slice of pizza, maybe. Do you have time?"

"I can't," he said. "I have to get home and watch Tristan and Caitlin now."

"Oh." I'd met his little brother and sister once before. They were really cute. "Well, maybe tonight? Or maybe I could go with you," I said. "I think we really need to talk."

"Yeah. Well, I really have to get home. I'm kind of late," Jake said quickly. He brushed past me and took off down the sidewalk towards his red Jeep.

I stared after him, my pulse drumming in my head. Why wouldn't he give me a chance?

I wanted to run after him, to make him listen to me. But I stopped myself. There was no point in chasing after him. Jake still didn't want to talk to me – and there was no way I could change his mind.

Brittany crossed the grass to where I stood frozen in place. "Tell me that wasn't as bad as it looked," she said.

I faced her, blinking back tears. "He totally blew me off," I told her. "A week ago we were so happy together, and now—"

Brittany threw an arm around my shoulders. "This is not right," she said. "Maybe Jake's not the guy you thought he was. Maybe you should move on."

But I didn't want to move on. I still wanted to get back together with Jake. And I wasn't going to give up on us – not yet!

"So what's happening with the party of the year?" Ben asked as we walked out of the CD store in the mall on Monday afternoon. Right after our driving lesson we'd caught the bus over. Ben switched his bag of CDs from his right hand to his left, and then reached for my hand.

"We still have a few things to figure out," I admitted. "Like where to have the party! We've got seventeen days. But who's counting?"

"Wait – isn't it at your house?" Ben asked.

"It was going to be," I said. "But now it isn't."

"Well, where are you thinking of having it?" Ben asked.

"We don't even know!" I confessed. "But don't tell anyone. We want people to think the party location is a big secret. Promise?"

"I won't tell anyone," Ben swore.

"We're meeting with Wilson tomorrow – he's going to give us some ideas." We rounded the corner to the food court. "Hey!" I cried as I spotted Lauren. She was sitting in a chair, sipping a soda, a shopping bag at her feet. Her long, wavy brown hair was wrapped up into a bun, held together with a pencil.

"Hey, guys!" Lauren said. "What are you up to?"

"About twenty-eight dollars so far." Ben gestured to the bag with CDs he was holding. "Plus tax."

Lauren and I both laughed. "We were thinking about getting some frozen yogurt," I told Lauren. "Do you want us to get you anything?"

"You guys hang out," Ben offered. "I'll get the frozen yogurt. Do you want something, Lauren?"

"Just water, if that's okay," she said.

"Gee, I don't know if I can afford that." Ben grinned. He went to the yogurt counter and waited in line. I took a seat across from Lauren.

"You know what?" Lauren leaned back in her chair. "Ben is the nicest guy."

"Yeah, he is," I agreed.

I gazed at Ben as he stood in line. "And he's definitely cute," I said.

"You're so lucky you ended up in that drivers' ed class together," Lauren said. "It's like . . . fate."

I thought about it for a second. "Fate." That was a word people used when they were talking about finding the love of their lives. Was Ben the love of my life? We'd been dating for about a month, but I wasn't sure.

"And it's so perfect how Mary-Kate found Jake, and then right afterwards, you found Ben – you know?" Lauren asked.

I nodded in agreement.

"Speaking of Mary-Kate and Jake . . . are they talking yet?" Lauren asked.

"No, and it's awful," I said. "She's so miserable. I mean, she thinks about him *all* the time. Have you seen her notebooks? They're covered with Jake's name!"

"She's totally crazy about him." Lauren sighed. "Just like you and Ben. It's so romantic."

I glanced up as Ben walked back towards our table. *He's great, but I don't think about him day and night*, I realised. My notebooks were full of class notes and to-do lists, not Ben's name surrounded by hearts. I didn't e-mail him twenty times a day the way Mary-Kate and Jake did before their fight. Mary-Kate said her heart did flip-flops every time she saw Jake. When I saw Ben, I felt fine – but no flip-flops. No nothing.

Mary-Kate and I aren't exactly alike, I told myself. *So maybe we don't act the same about boyfriends. We're different, that's all.*

But a little alarm went off in the back of my mind: *What if I'm trying to convince myself that I'm crazy about Ben – but I'm really not?*

What if he's not the guy for me after all?

chapter five

"It's great to see you guys again," Wilson said. "Even if it is kind of an emergency."

Ashley and I sat down across from Wilson's big oak desk on Tuesday afternoon. Dad had picked us up after I got home from my driving lesson. He waited outside Wilson's office, doing business on his mobile. Wilson's office was in his house – a gorgeous Spanish-style ranch house.

Wilson himself was totally hip – in a post-college-guy sort of way. He was dressed in baggy cargos, a maroon T-shirt and a well-worn cream-coloured baseball cap.

"Let's get right down to it." Wilson pulled a sheet of paper out of a folder. "You have two weeks and two days until your party. I've made up a list of party locations that fit a hundred people *and* your budget *and* should be available on short notice."

He handed the sheet to me, and I promptly handed it to Ashley. After all, she's the organised one.

"This is so awesome!" I said. "Thanks."

"Do you think we can find a place in such a short amount of time?" Ashley asked.

"Definitely. Just remember – you have a limited budget. So if some of these places don't seem perfect, don't focus on their flaws – think about their potential. With some window-dressing and the right lighting, any place can look amazing," Wilson said. He poured himself a glass of orange juice from the pitcher on his desk. "So, what information do you want to put on your new e-mail invitations?"

Ashley tapped her pen against her glittery purple notebook. "Well, we have a really good start." She opened the notebook and read out loud: "'Mary-Kate and Ashley's New and Improved Sweet Sixteen.'"

Wilson raised his eyebrows, as if he were waiting for more. "Go on," he said.

"We can't," I said. "That's all we have."

Wilson laughed. "I like it." He took off his cap and ran his hand through his long blond hair. "But it doesn't say much, because we don't have much to say. Not until you know where the party will be, right?"

"Right," I agreed. "That's the problem. So we

need to say something that *sounds* exciting. Something that sounds as if we know exactly what we're doing—"

"—but not actually say anything at all!" Ashley finished.

"Ah, the fine art of publicity," Wilson said.

"How about 'Mary-Kate and Ashley's New and Improved Sweet Sixteen. Hot new location!'" I began, thinking hard. "'Hot new guests! Watch your e-mail for more details.'"

"That's great!" Ashley said.

"Excellent," Wilson agreed. "So we have new invitations. You're working on finding a new place for the party. There's just one more problem."

"There is?" Ashley said.

"Have you made up a list of the boys you're going to invite?" Wilson asked.

Ashley glanced at the to-do list in her notebook. "I have that written down here. Really."

"Why don't you tackle it tonight?" Wilson suggested. "You'll want to invite the guys as soon as possible, so they can set aside the date."

"Right!" Ashley put a star next to that item in her notebook.

I smiled nervously. There was only one boy I wanted on the guest list: Jake. If you subtracted Ben, that left forty-eight boys we needed to invite. Did we even *know* forty-eight boys?

• • •

"What about Brandon – that guy two houses down?" I asked. "I mean, he's always been nice to us.

How many would that make?" Mary-Kate asked me.

We were in my bedroom on Wednesday night. I was sitting at the computer, entering the names as we thought of them. "That makes twenty-three," I told her.

"Okay. So there's Mark from the drama club," Mary-Kate said.

"Mark?" I asked.

"Yeah. The one we met when we were acting in the play last year. He was the . . . um . . . assistant director or something," Mary-Kate said. "Remember how funny he was? He'd be great at a party."

"I think you mean Mike. He was the stage manager," I reminded her. "And he moved. He doesn't go to our school any more."

"Oh. So that's why I haven't seen him around." Mary-Kate frowned. "All right. Let me think. There's always Melvin."

"Melvin? You mean our third cousin Melvin, whose idea of fun is playing video games for seven hours straight?" I asked in horror. "No way! We're not *that* desperate."

"We're not?" Mary-Kate asked. "Because it kind of seemed like we were. I mean, *I* can't think of anyone else. Unless we invite everyone in school, which seems very second-grade to me, like when we gave our whole class valentines."

"Tacky," I agreed.

"Exactly," Mary-Kate said.

"We don't know enough boys – you're right," I admitted. "But if we asked our friends about boys *they* know, I bet we'd come up with more than enough." Then it hit me – that was the perfect thing to do. Ask for assistance – in our new invitations!

I jumped out of my chair. "Brainstorm!" I yelled. I leaped on to my bed and started jumping up and down on it.

"What?" Mary-Kate stared at me as if I'd just sprouted another head. "What is it?"

"We can make it a Sadie Hawkins party!" I said. "Our theme is girl power, right? Well, it's a girl power thing to ask a guy out instead of waiting for him to ask you, isn't it?"

Mary-Kate shrugged. "Sure."

"So this is just like another twist on the theme. And if everyone we already invited brings a date, or a friend, then there will be a totally equal number of boys and girls at our party," I explained, "just like we want there to be."

"Hey – that's a *brilliant* idea!" Mary-Kate cried. She climbed on to the bed and started to jump beside me.

Yikes! The bed groaned, then lurched a little to one side, as if it were about to collapse.

I laughed. "Maybe we're getting too old for this." We both got off the bed and sat back down at my desk.

"First things first," I said. I deleted our list of boys to invite. Then I opened a new e-mail and typed in the announcement about our party and its secret location. We told everyone to watch her e-mail for further announcements. Then we said that in keeping with our girl power theme, everyone should invite the guy of her choice to the party, whether as a date or as a friend.

"Done!" I quickly read the message over for typos and pressed the Send button.

"Great. Now we just have to find a place to *put* everyone." I heard a flicker of anxiety in Mary-Kate's voice. "Or there won't *be* any party!"

"We've got to work fast," I agreed. "I'll start on Wilson's list tomorrow afternoon while you're at your driving lesson. Mom promised to drive me around to check out a few of the places. She said she wants to help out as much as she can, since the party will be our only present this year."

"Yeah – right." Mary-Kate laughed. "I don't believe that for a second. The more she says that, the more sure I am that it isn't true."

"I don't know," I protested. "They seem pretty serious about it."

"Ashley, did you *see* Dad's face when I asked about it? He was redder than a tomato," Mary-Kate said. "Mom and Dad love playing this game with us every year. I think they're just trying to throw us off the trail."

"Well, in that case . . . where should we look first?" I asked.

Mary-Kate grinned. "Mom and Dad aren't home," she said. "It's a perfect chance to check the birthday closet."

There was a closet in the basement that Mom and Dad had used before to hide our birthday gifts. They locked the door, of course, but we knew where they hid the key – on top of the water heater. They just didn't know that we knew.

We sneaked downstairs, even though no one was home to catch us. I shoved Dad's big toolbox across the floor to the water heater. Then I stepped on it and felt around for the key.

"Got it!" I whispered, handing the key to Mary-Kate.

"We probably shouldn't be doing this." Mary-Kate slipped the key into the lock and slowly pushed the door open. "But it's a tradition, right?"

"Right." I flicked on the light switch. "Uh-oh."

The closet was completely empty – except for a large neon-pink piece of poster board with the words NICE TRY! written on it in black marker.

"They're on to us!" I cried. "They know we've looked here before!"

"Yeah, but this means they *are* giving us a present," Mary-Kate said. "Come on. That's enough snooping for one day."

We trooped back upstairs. Mary-Kate stopped in the kitchen for a snack. I went to my room. Wilson's list of party places lay on my desk, glowing in the light from my computer screen.

We'd better find something tomorrow, I thought, staring at the list. *Or we'll have one hundred party guests all dressed up with nowhere to go!*

chapter six

"Is this it, Ashley?" Mom asked. She pulled the car into a big crowded parking lot on Thursday afternoon.

I reread the address on the piece of paper in my lap. "This is it," I told her. "The last place on Wilson's list. Pizza Pals."

I glanced through the windshield, and my heart sank. A huge statue of a green dinosaur stood guard outside the restaurant. The words PREHISTORIC PIZZA PAL were painted on its belly. A Pals Playground with seesaws and a slide stood on the right side of the restaurant.

"What do you think, honey?" Mom asked.

"This isn't exactly the image we were going for," I complained. "It's a kiddie restaurant!"

The last two places hadn't been much better – we'd seen a sports and recreation centre that smelled like chlorine, and an old warehouse space that was cool-looking but a little too grungy for Mom's taste.

Before that, Mom and I had visited three other restaurants, a bowling alley and a botanical garden. The garden was beautiful, but there were several restrictions on what we could do if we had our party there. The biggest problem was that dancing wasn't allowed. I couldn't see having our sweet sixteen without dancing to celebrate!

Then again, maybe I can live without dancing, I thought as the Pizza Pals dinosaur loomed above me.

"Uh, Mom?" I said as we got out of the car. "I'm not sure if we need to go inside. I mean, this pretty much says it all." I tapped the dinosaur with my fingers.

"Well, it might be a little young, but remember – Wilson can transform a place," Mom said. "He wouldn't have put it on the list if he didn't think it was appropriate."

"Appropriate for what?" I muttered under my breath as we walked through the front door. "A kindergarten graduation?"

"Welcome to Pizza Pals!" A teenage girl wearing overalls and a striped T-shirt greeted us.

"Uh, thanks," I said, smiling at her.

"Hi, we'd like to talk to someone about renting your banquet room," Mom said with a polite smile. "Is the manager available?"

"You betcha!" she said. "Be right back." She zipped away on rollerskates.

"Mom, maybe we should think this over," I said. "Are you sure we can't fit a hundred people into our house?"

"Ashley, you've got to consider all your options." Mom looked around at all the families in the dining room. "You know, it sure is popular here!"

"With little kids," I said. I glanced at a clown entertaining a table of small children at a birthday party. Half of them were yelling, and the other half were crying. *Please let the banquet room be booked on June 13*, I thought. *I'll die if I have to have my party here!*

A minute or so later, the clown came over to me and Mom. "Hello, I'm Rick, the manager. I understand you're interested in renting the Pals Party Room?"

"Yes. This is for my daughters' sweet sixteen party," Mom said. "Would the room be available on June thirteenth?"

"Let me check." Rick went behind the host stand and flipped through a calendar.

I crossed my fingers. *Please say no. Please say no.*

"You're in luck!" Rick told us. "It's available."

"Great," I said. So much for crossing fingers.

"Let me show you the Pals Party Room, and if

43

you like it, you can put down a deposit to hold the room."

The only way we'll have our party here is if the restaurant is completely closed for the night, I thought as I tripped over a balloon. *And the clown called in sick.* But deep down I knew that this place was our last hope.

The banquet room wasn't as bad as I'd expected. It didn't have any personality at all, but that was okay – we could add all the decorations and flavour ourselves. There were several round tables, and a large open space that could be used for dancing.

"We have another entrance at the back here, so it's completely separate from the restaurant. And you can bring your own flowers, candles, et cetera. You can have it catered, or we can provide all the pizza you can eat," Rick explained. "And there's plenty of atmosphere if you plan on dancing." He pointed to the ceiling, where a sad and lonely-looking silver disco ball hung without moving. "You young kids love to dance, right?"

"Right," I said slowly. This place *could* work – in the sense that we could completely change it around to make it what we want. But . . .

"What do you think, Ashley?" Mom asked.

A vision flashed before my eyes – the elegant sweet sixteen I had always dreamed of. Girls in ball gowns, boys in tuxedos, flowers and candles everywhere . . .

Then I faced the reality. A bare room in a pizza place.

I didn't want to admit it, but it was the best place we'd seen so far. If you could forget about the rollerskating waitresses and the giant dinosaur.

But then, everyone would be pulling into the Pizza Pals parking lot . . .

"I guess it might be okay." I groaned, not believing the words coming out of my mouth.

"I think so, too," Mom said. "I mean, it's not perfect, but it will fit your budget. And you really need to reserve a place now."

I pulled Mom aside. "Mom, I've been dreaming about my sweet sixteen since I was twelve," I whispered. "And this place . . . well, it doesn't fit in with my dream!"

Mom frowned. "I'm sorry, Ashley, but the party is two weeks away! The caterer needs to know where the party will be, not to mention your guests—"

"I'll make a deal with you," I offered. "If I can find a better place, we'll switch. But if I can't find something else in time, we'll have the party here. Okay?"

Mom thought it over. "On one condition," she said. She turned to the clown. "Excuse me, Rick. Is the deposit refundable?"

"Yes, of course," he said. "We just need three days' advance notice."

Mom turned back to me. "All right. We've got a deal. We'll reserve this now. If you can't find something else, the party will be here."

I bit my lip. *We are not having the party here,* I vowed. *I'll do everything I can to make sure of that!*

"Okay, Mary-Kate, you'll want to take a right at the next street," Ms. Junger instructed.

I flicked on the indicator and pulled the wheel to the right.

"Nicely done," Ms. Junger said. "We'll stay on this street for a few blocks."

"Okay – no problem." I kept driving along, enjoying being behind the wheel. But I couldn't help wondering how Ashley and Mom were doing. How many places had they seen so far? Had Ashley chosen one yet?

Hey, we could have a primo party spot already! I thought, my excitement rising. *Ashley could be standing in the perfect place at this very moment!*

"Take a right here," Ms. Junger instructed after we had been driving for a few minutes.

I signalled my turn and followed her instruction.

I had to pay close attention to the street signs

because I wasn't familiar with this section of town. I didn't know anyone who lived over here – not that I could think of, anyway. It was pretty, though, with lots of tall palm trees and winding streets.

"And turn left here," Ms. Junger said. I put on the indicator and glanced to the left. There, striding down the sidewalk, was a guy who looked exactly like Jake.

I gasped. *Hold on a second*, I thought as I peered out of the window. *That* is *Jake!*

"Left, Mary-Kate," Ms. Junger said. "Turn left here."

What was Jake doing *here*? I wondered. He didn't have any friends who lived in this neighbourhood.

"Mary-Kate, you missed that turn, so take the *next* left," Ms. Junger said.

I nodded at Ms. Junger's words, but I didn't actually hear them. My mind kept racing. If Jake didn't have any friends in this area, maybe he was here for another reason – and there was only one I could think of. Maybe he was here to see a new girlfriend—

"Stop here. Mary-Kate are you listening? Mary-Kate, stop. *Stop!*" Ms. Junger ordered me.

The car screeched to a halt. I broke out of my trance and stared at Ms. Junger. I winced, realising that she had stepped on the dual brake.

"Pull over here and we'll switch drivers," Ms. Junger said. "I told you to turn left twice and you didn't. You're not paying attention at all!"

Jerry, my classmate in the back seat, muttered, "Uh-oh," under his breath.

"I – I *was*," I said, "but just then I saw something, um, bizarre, and so . . ."

I pulled towards the curb. Ms. Junger told Jerry and me to trade places.

I got out of the car and glanced around. Jake was gone.

I climbed into the back seat and stared out of the window, watching for him.

We were nowhere near his neighbourhood. I racked my brain, trying to come up with some reason why Jake would be here. But my mind kept going back to the same thing. There was only one explanation that made sense.

He must be seeing another girl, I thought. *That's why he doesn't want to talk to me! Here I am, completely miserable over him, and he's already dating someone else!*

Tears pricked the backs of my eyelids. *That's crazy,* I told myself. *How could he have found someone else so soon?*

But what if my crazy thought was true? What if Jake really did have a new girlfriend?

chapter seven

I dropped my tray on to the cafeteria table Friday at lunchtime. "Have either of you guys heard that Jake has a new girlfriend?" Brittany, Lauren and Ashley stared up at me.

"Mary-Kate, what are you talking about?" Brittany asked. "Jake with a new girlfriend? Since when?"

"No way." Lauren shook her head. "He wouldn't. He couldn't."

"And what makes you think he *does*?" Brittany asked.

"Okay. Ashley's already heard this, but when I was taking my driving lesson yesterday, I *saw* Jake." I explained how I'd completely missed Ms. Junger's instructions because I was so busy watching Jake walk down the sidewalk. "He doesn't live anywhere near that neighbourhood," I said. "Why else would he be there?"

"Mary-Kate, come on," Brittany said. "He could have been out for a walk. Or visiting his grandmother. Or selling magazine subscriptions door to door. I mean, there are a dozen explanations that *don't* involve him having a new girlfriend."

"That's what *I* tried to tell her." Ashley sighed.

"I haven't heard anything around school, either," Lauren said. "But I guess you could always ask Todd Malone if you wanted to find out. He and Jake are good friends."

I wished I could ask Todd – I was dying to find out the truth. But Todd might tell Jake that I'd asked. "No way!" I groaned. "Then I'd look even more pathetic."

"Look, Jake does *not* have a new girlfriend," Brittany declared. "You guys are going to get back together. Just wait."

"I *hate* waiting," I wailed.

"We know," Brittany, Lauren and Ashley all chirped at the same time.

I laughed for the first time that day. Okay, so I can be a little impatient sometimes. Anybody would be in my place if she thought her boyfriend was seeing another girl. Especially if she liked him as much as I liked Jake. I couldn't relax until I found out the truth.

Lauren leaned across the table and whispered, "Have you guys decided where you're having the party yet?"

Ashley glanced around to make sure no one was eavesdropping. "I saw a bunch of places yesterday," she whispered. "But nothing was really *right*."

"Something had better be right soon," Brittany said. "You guys, there are less than two weeks until your party!"

"I know," I groaned. "We have to choose a place *now*."

"Mom put down a deposit at this place called Pizza Pals, but we're not having the party there unless we absolutely have to," Ashley said.

"Pizza Pals? Is that the place with the giant dinosaur out front and the skating waiters?" Lauren asked.

I held up my hand. "Please. Don't remind me."

"At least we have appointments to get our hair and nails done on our birthday," Ashley said. "And our dresses are ready – all the alterations are done!"

"Oh, yeah. That's great. Except you won't have a place to *wear* them unless you get moving," Brittany commented.

"Stop!" I tossed a french fry on to her tray. "We will have a place. Soon." I looked at Ashley and smiled. "Right?"

"Right. Sure." She smiled back at me. "And we'll pass our driving tests. And then we'll, you know . . . create world peace. In our spare time."

• • •

Ashley and I were walking down the hallway towards our lockers at the end of lunch period, when we ran into Melanie Han and Tashema Mitchell.

"Hey you guys, we're *so* excited about your party!" Melanie said.

"Getting updates by e-mail is so cool. How'd you come up with that idea?" Tashema asked.

"Oh, it just, um . . . came to us," I said.

"It's awesome. When's the next update?" Melanie asked.

"Soon." Ashley nudged me with her elbow. "But we can't tell you when, because that would ruin the surprise."

"I can't wait to find out where this party is," Tashema said.

I covered my mouth to stifle a laugh. *Neither can we!* I thought.

"Can't you give us a clue? A teensy tiny clue?" Tashema begged. "I want to pick out what I'm going to wear, and I need to make sure it's right."

"We'll be sending out another update in the next couple of days – so just keep checking your e-mail," Ashley said. "We'll give you plenty of advance notice, don't worry."

"Okay, cool." Melanie waved to us.

"I'm going to check it every hour, on the hour," Tashema said before she and Melanie walked off.

"Sounds like our plan is working great!" I said to Ashley. "No one suspects a thing!" We turned the corner at the end of the hall and nearly crashed right into Rachel Adams, who was walking towards us.

"Hey, Mary-Kate and Ashley. I got your invitation – thanks!" she said.

"You're welcome," I replied. Rachel was a good friend of mine from when I played on the basketball team. "Can you come?"

"I'll be there for sure – and I *love* your Sadie Hawkins idea. I'm inviting tons of boys, so we should have enough guys to dance with and . . ."

I turned and looked at Ashley, whose face had gone completely pale. "Um, did you just say you're inviting tons of boys?" I asked Rachel. "You were supposed to invite only one."

Rachel looked confused. "But your e-mail invite. It said to invite *guys*. Plural. So I thought I'd invite the guys' basketball team for a start. Then I thought of asking my older brother if he'd come and bring a couple of his friends, because some of them are really cute."

"Yeah, um, that sounds great!" Ashley said as she pulled me away. "I'm sorry, Rachel, but we have to run now. See you later!"

Ashley and I hurried down the hall. "We *didn't*," I groaned as we broke into a run.

"We *couldn't* have," Ashley said. We raced into

the computer lab and grabbed a seat at one of the terminals. Ashley signed on to her e-mail account in record time. She pulled up her 'sent mail'. Suddenly, there it was on the screen: our latest e-mail invitation. Ashley ran her finger along the invitation's text until she got to the important line:

"Please invite the guys of your choice."

"*Guys* – plural!" Ashley wailed.

Several heads popped up from behind computer monitors as people strained to see what was going on.

"Shh," a couple of people said.

"Oh no. The entire school is going to come to our party now. The entire city. The entire *world*!" Ashley whispered. "What are we going to do?"

chapter eight

"Mary-Kate, we should be out looking for party places," I complained later that afternoon. "Or we'll be stuck with Pizza Pals!"

The two of us stopped in front of a storefront window with MENU BY MARGO printed on the glass. Wilson had hired Margo to cater our party.

"This is important, too," Mary-Kate insisted, opening the door. "No matter where the party is, we're having at least a hundred guests. And Margo thinks we're having only fifty. We've got to let her know what's going on."

"Good afternoon, may I help you?" Margo asked, coming out of the kitchen. Her green chef's apron was dusted with flour.

"Hi." Mary-Kate smiled. "We booked you to cater our party on June thirteenth. I'm Mary-Kate Olsen, and this is Ashley."

"Of course!" Margo nodded. "You're having the sweet sixteen party at your house, aren't you?"

"Right . . ." I began. "At least, that *was* the plan."

"Oh, really? What's changed?" Margo asked.

"Well, we can't have it at our house any more because we changed the number of guests. We were scheduled for a sit-down dinner for fifty, but now we have a *hundred* people coming to our party. We can't spend any more money on the food. So we're here to ask – do you think you'll still be able to cater the party for us?"

"Are you joking?" Margo said.

I held my breath. Was Margo going to cancel on us?

"Of course we can," she finished. "People's guest lists change all the time."

I let out a huge sigh. "Even though the party's less than two weeks away?"

"Sure. We'll just change the menu around to make it work. We're very flexible here – we have to be," Margo said. "Would you mind coming into the kitchen with me to talk about it? I'm on a tight deadline today."

Mary-Kate and I followed her to a large counter, where she was decorating a collection of tiny cheesecakes – each one with a different pattern on top. She was using orange and green icing to draw a carrot on one of them. "So, we've still got a couple of weeks, which is plenty of time. I've had people completely change their parties two *days* ahead of time. For now, you're thinking about a hundred, though?"

Mary-Kate nodded. "We hope it won't be bigger than that."

"Right. And is the party still going to be at your house?"

"No," I told her. "We haven't found a place to have it yet."

Margo stopped decorating the cheesecake and turned to us. "Now, that *is* a problem."

I cringed. "We're working on it."

"My staff and I need to know as soon as possible, so we can be prepared," Margo said.

"I understand," Mary-Kate said. "And we'll get it locked up really, really soon – we promise."

Margo nodded. "Good. In the meantime, let's think about the menu." She started decorating another mini-cheesecake. "For a big party it's fun to have different food stations, each decorated to go with the theme of the food. Your guests could travel between, say, a Mexican beach hut, where we'll be grilling chicken and veggie fajitas, and a Japanese sushi bar, and a New Orleans carnival stand with Cajun crawfish and gumbo – like that."

"Cool," I said, my mouth watering at the thought of all the food she'd just described.

"That really sounds like fun!" Mary-Kate commented. "And way too nice for the Pizza Pals banquet room," she added.

"Pizza Pals? What's that?" Margo asked.

"Just this place we're considering having the party," I said. "We don't like it that much, though."

"You know, if our friends invite too many guys, Pizza Pals won't be big enough for the party," Mary-Kate said. "There won't *be* a place big enough. We'll just have to pitch a tent on the beach and hope for the best!"

My eyes widened as I pictured the scene. A bonfire in the sand, dancing by the surf, the sunset over the ocean . . . "Mary-Kate – that's a brilliant idea! We can have the party in a tent on the beach!"

"We can?" Mary-Kate asked.

"Sure. We'll rent one of those giant white tents, and we can set it up right near the ocean. And if there are too many people to fit under the tent, then they'll just spill out on to the beach," I explained.

Margo nodded. "Your sister's right. It's an excellent idea – if you can pull it off in time."

"Do you know how much it would cost?" I asked her.

"Well, the beach is public property, and the tents are not that expensive. We might even have a few brochures from a tent rental company out front," Margo offered. "Now – I hate to cut this short, but I've really got to focus or I'm going to have ten very burned chickens. Keep in touch, girls – give us the location as soon as you can!"

"We will, I promise. Thanks so much!" I told her.

Mary-Kate and I couldn't get home fast enough. Our new party plan was ultracool. We couldn't wait to let everyone know about it. We had to send out the next party update!

"Give me another line from the brochure," I told Ashley.

Ashley peered at the tent rental flyer Margo had given us. We'd called them and found out that renting a tent was well within our budget. "'There's no better party decoration than the sun setting over the ocean.'"

"Hmm." I stared at my computer screen. I was writing an e-mail giving more details about the party. I wanted to whet everyone's appetite without giving too much away.

"Mary-Kate and Ashley Party Update," I typed. "The official location is a very cool place. Music: the sound of the crashing surf. Decorations: a view of the sun setting over the ocean. Stay tuned for exact location at a later date!"

Ashley read the e-mail over my shoulder. "That's good," she said.

I sent the e-mail to everyone on our list. "There. Everyone will be so psyched when they find out the location is the beach!"

Ashley leaned back on my bed and rested her head against the pillows with a contented sigh. "Isn't this great?" she said. "We're so close to being done. And everything's finally working out."

I rested my chin on the back of my desk chair. "We can just relax and start thinking about the easy stuff now."

Ashley raised her eyebrow. "Like passing our driving tests next week?"

I sighed. "And getting Jake back. I guess things aren't exactly easy yet." The phone rang, and I grabbed it from my dresser. "Hello?"

"Mary-Kate, is that you?"

"Hey, Wilson," I said. "How are you? *Where* are you?"

"Flying over Vegas, but never mind about that. Did you figure out—" he started to ask.

"Wilson, you won't believe it," I interrupted, "but we figured out *everything*." I explained about meeting with Margo, and how I'd got the idea to have the party on the beach. "We checked into renting a tent, and it's totally within our budget. Isn't that awesome?"

"Yeah, it sounds great," Wilson agreed.

"We thought so, too! So we sent out another update and—"

"But it would have been better if you'd thought of it a month ago," Wilson interrupted me. "Then we would have had time to get the permit you need to have a party on the beach."

"What?" I yelped.

"I'm sorry, girls. It's too late. We can't have the party on the beach, no matter how cool it would be."

I quickly tossed the phone to Ashley and sat back down at my computer. "Isn't there some way to unsend messages?" I asked. "Delete! Stop! Return to sender!" I cried as I clicked the mouse in every possible place.

But the message was gone.

And what was worse, we already had a reply from Melanie Han. "Sounds great – I love the surf – keep me posted!"

Ashley hung up the phone. "Wilson told me about the permit. He also said we should take another look at Pizza Pals because we'd be surprised at how much could be done with decorations." She groaned. "If we end up at that Pizza Pals place after we sent that e-mail . . ."

"We won't," I said. "We *can't*. We have thirteen days to find somewhere else. That's what we're going to do!"

chapter nine

"What did Ben think of the whole tent-on-the-beach fiasco?" Mary-Kate asked me on Saturday afternoon. We took our change from the Starbucks cashier and headed for a table.

"Ben?" I stopped in the middle of the room. A tall woman brushed past me. "What do you mean?"

"Didn't you tell him about it?" Mary-Kate asked.

"No," I replied. "I haven't spoken to him since drivers' ed last Wednesday."

Mary-Kate gave me a funny look. Then she pointed out an empty table and headed for it.

"Why?" I asked, taking a seat. "Do you think that's weird?"

"No," Mary-Kate said. "It's just . . . I don't know. When I was with Jake we talked or e-mailed about ten times a day. I wanted to tell him every little thing that happened. But maybe it's different, since

Ben doesn't go to the same school as we do . . ."

"I tell Ben lots of things," I said. "I'll get around to telling him all about it eventually."

But at the time it happened, it never occurred to me to tell him, I realised. When things happened to me, good or bad, Ben usually wasn't the first person I thought of calling.

Does that mean I'm not crazy enough about him? I wondered. *Does it mean I shouldn't be going out with him?* I considered asking Mary-Kate what she thought, but she changed the subject.

"I hate to bring up another decision we have to make," she said. "But what shoes are we going to wear with our cool new dresses?"

She carefully draped the dresses over an empty chair. We'd just picked them up, with the final alterations done. They looked better than ever now that they fitted us perfectly.

"How can you worry about *shoes* at a time like this?" I said. "We don't even know where we're having the party!"

"Maybe not, but we can't go barefoot," she joked. "We've already been through the beach concept, remember?"

I smiled, glad that Mary-Kate could keep her sense of humour about it. I reached into my bag and pulled out my glittery purple notebook. I glanced through the appointment section.

"I have a day set aside in our schedule next week to get all our accessories," I announced. "And in the meantime, we need to go over something more important – the final guest list. That way we can stop by Margo's on the way home, and confirm the total number of guests."

The day before was the final RSVP date. We'd spent the evening reading e-mails, answering the phone and opening mailed replies.

"Well, the good news is that it looks like we're coming in right on target," I said.

"Which target is that?" Mary-Kate asked. "Because let's face it, we've missed a lot of them lately." She unwrapped her straw and stuck it into her grande Frappuccino.

"Almost everyone has sent their RSVP, and we have a total of ninety-eight guests. Which leaves room for a couple more people," I said.

"Hold on – how did *that* work out?" Mary-Kate asked. "What about Rachel inviting the entire boys' basketball team?"

"Oh, she still invited them," I told her. "But a lot of girls decided *not* to ask a guy. Some people are totally happy coming without dates – which is very cool. Especially at a girl power party." I smiled as I reached for my coffee drink.

"And some people are totally *unhappy* coming by themselves," Mary-Kate said glumly. I followed her gaze to a couple sitting at a small table by the window. The girl had long blonde hair, and her boyfriend had short brown hair. They looked a lot like Mary-Kate and Jake – except for three things: (1) They were together, (2) they were holding hands as they talked and sipped from their mugs, and (3) they looked happy.

"Come on, Mary-Kate. Don't give up yet," I said.

"I know you're still upset about Jake, but I think we have a lot to celebrate," I said. "We have our dresses, and they look completely awesome. We have everyone at school talking about our party. We have our final guest list—"

"Ashley!" she interrupted. "Don't you understand? None of this matters if we don't have a place to hold the party!"

"I know," I said, a little hurt. I guessed she hadn't kept her sense of humour so well after all. "I'm just trying to think positively, that's all."

She sighed, pushing her cup in circles on the table. "I'm sorry. I'm just feeling stressed out today."

"I'm stressed, too," I confessed. "But I'm even more worried about my driving test next week."

"What do you mean? Getting our licences is going to be so cool!" she said.

"Easy for you to say. You're totally great at driving." I stirred my coffee. "I'm not. You should have seen me at my lessons this past week. And we get only one more!"

"I'm sure you're better than you think," she told me. "And we'll be there together, so don't worry."

"Don't worry about what?" someone behind me asked.

I turned and saw Theresa standing with Todd Malone, her boyfriend. I'd met Ben at one of Todd's parties. And Mary-Kate had danced with Jake for the first time at the same party.

I glanced at Mary-Kate's face, wondering if she was thinking about that night.

"Ashley's worried about her driving test," Mary-Kate told them. "We're taking it next week."

"It'll be easy – don't sweat it," Todd commented.

"Did you guys get my RSVP?" Theresa asked.

"Yeah, we did – thanks," I said. "And you're bringing—"

"Well, I'm not totally sure who's coming with me," Theresa said, glancing at Todd.

"What?" Todd asked. "What do you mean? *I* am."

"Don't count on it," Theresa said. She laughed and put her arm around Todd's waist. "I haven't asked you yet."

"Ha-ha," Todd said, rolling his eyes.

Theresa and Todd totally like each other, I thought, watching them. *Do Ben and I look that way when we're together?*

"Are you guys inviting dates?" Theresa asked

Mary-Kate and me. "Let me guess – Ashley's bringing Ben, and Mary-Kate . . ."

Her voice trailed off, and her face went red. I could tell she'd suddenly remembered that Jake and Mary-Kate had broken up.

"I don't have a date yet," Mary-Kate said. "But that's okay." She tried to smile, but I knew she felt miserable about it inside.

"Yeah. Well, we should probably get going," Todd said. "We just wanted to say hi."

They turned to leave, but then Theresa stopped. "Mary-Kate, I'm really sorry about you and Jake breaking up," she said. "I know for a fact that he still likes you."

"See you guys around!" Todd called. He gently pulled Theresa out of Starbucks and on to the sidewalk. She turned around to wave at us.

Mary-Kate looked shocked. "What is Jake's problem?" she asked to me. "If he still likes me, the way Theresa says, then why won't he talk to me?"

"I don't know, Mary-Kate," I said. "But we have got to find out."

chapter ten

"So, thanks for the movie." I looked into Ben's dark brown eyes on Sunday night. *He's going to kiss me,* I realised.

For some reason, I found myself edging away from him. "I'll . . . umm . . . see you tomorrow."

I moved towards my house. *What are you doing?* I asked myself. *Don't you want Ben to kiss you?*

"It's my mom, isn't it?" Ben asked. I peeked over his shoulder. His mother was waiting in the car. She had dropped us off at the movies and picked us up afterwards. "She kills the mood, right?" Ben continued.

That must be it! I thought. *I just don't want to kiss him in front of his mother. Of course!*

I peered at Ben's mother sitting in the driver's seat, trying not to look as if she was watching us. "Yeah, it *is* kind of a problem," I said.

"That's cool. I understand. Well, good night, Ashley." Ben gave me a quick hug and walked away..

"Good night," I said. "And thanks for going out tonight – I had a really nice time!" I smiled and waved as he and his mother pulled out of the driveway.

I *did* have a nice time with Ben – so why didn't I want to kiss him good night? The first time we'd kissed, at the party on the houseboat, it had felt amazing. What was my problem?

His mother was watching us! I reminded myself as I unlocked the door and walked into our house. Who would want to kiss under those circumstances?

I headed for the kitchen to get myself a glass of milk. I tossed my denim jacket on to the back of a chair and opened the refrigerator.

Once I had poured my glass of milk, I turned off the kitchen light and headed for the stairs. Then I noticed something bobbing on the hallway wall, by the closet at the bottom of the stairs. It looked like a flashlight beam.

Wait a second, I thought. *Why is someone walking around my house with a flashlight?* There was only one answer that came to mind – and I didn't like it. Were we being *robbed*? I knew Mom and Dad had gone out to a work function, which meant Mary-Kate should have been home by herself.

"H-hello?" I said. Then I cleared my throat and tried to sound older – and bigger. "Who's there?"

I crawled out from behind a stack of boxes in the storage closet. *Nope. Nothing here, either*! This entire present search was turning out to be yet another bust.

"I said, who's there?" a voice demanded.

I gasped and pointed my flashlight in the direction of the voice. The beam landed right on Ashley's face! "Ashley, it's me!" I said.

Ashley shielded her eyes from the light. "Mary-Kate, stop shining that in my face!"

"Oh – sorry." I hopped out of the overcrowded closet and flicked on the hall light switch.

"What were you doing? You scared me," Ashley said.

"I was bored, so I started looking for our presents again."

"In the dark?" Ashley asked.

"In case Mom and Dad came home," I answered. "I didn't want them to see the light on in the storage closet and find out what I was doing."

"And?" Ashley said. "Did you find anything?"

I shook my head. "Not unless you count dust bunnies. How was your date?"

"Okay." Ashley shrugged and took a sip of milk from the glass she was holding. She didn't seem all that thrilled, which was strange. I decided she was just tired. Or maybe she needed to talk.

"Hey, that looks good." I pointed to her glass. "Want to hang out with me while I get some?" I asked.

"Sure," she said.

We went into the kitchen, and Ashley sat down at the kitchen table. "So. What did you do tonight?" she asked.

"Not much. Before Mom and Dad left for their party, I helped Mom make some cookies to take to the day care centre tomorrow. Then I asked Dad where our presents were hiding," I said. "And he blushed a lot, and said there weren't any, and then after they left I searched every room. Hey, it's better than doing homework."

"You seem like you're in a good mood," Ashley commented.

"I'm trying," I said. "But the problem is that every time I try to do my geometry homework, I think about how Jake helped me study for my last test and how much I like him." I sighed. "It's a vicious circle, which is why I'm not even *looking* at my geometry book tonight."

"I know it's not the same thing, but I can help you with geometry later, if you want," Ashley offered.

"Thanks," I said with a smile. "But you're right. It's not the same."

"I know you feel really bad right now – about Jake." Ashley sighed. "But at least you *know* how you feel about him."

"What do you mean?" I asked.

Ashley tucked her hair behind her ears. "It's Ben. I've been thinking. I've noticed the way you talk about Jake."

"And talk and talk and talk . . ." I joked.

She laughed. "Well, sort of. But that just shows how much you like him. Me, on the other hand . . . I like seeing Ben, when I see him. But I don't get all woozy, like you're supposed to when you fall in love."

"Good thing, because who wants to pass out on a date? Very embarrassing," I joked, wrinkling my nose.

"Come on, I'm serious!" Ashley pleaded. "There are ways you're supposed to feel when you're going out with someone – and I don't feel them. Isn't that weird?"

"Not really. Everyone's different," I said.

Ashley frowned. "I don't think that's it."

"Come on, you'll get used to being weird," I teased her. "I have."

"Mary-Kate, I'm serious." Ashley looked at me.

"Okay. Sorry," I apologised. "I am taking this seriously." I took a deep breath and let it out. "I guess I would say that everything you've told me could mean that Ben's not the right guy for you. Maybe he seemed like it at first, so that's why you went out with him."

"This is embarrassing, but to be honest? I think I might have started going out with Ben because I wanted to have a boyfriend – at the same time *you* had one," Ashley said.

"Really?" I was surprised. It wasn't like Ashley to do something just because I was doing it. Not at all. "But I remember when you met him – you really liked him."

"I still do. He's funny, and he always makes me laugh. He's cute. He's smart," I said.

"So what's the problem?" I asked.

Ashley shrugged. "It's fun. But it's not like you and Jake. There are fireworks when you and Jake are together."

"Correction – there *were* fireworks," I said. "Now there are ashes."

"Yikes," Ashley said.

"Sorry. I don't mean to be so dramatic." I looked across the table at Ashley. "But, if you really think you don't like Ben that way . . . you should tell him. And you should tell him soon, before he gets more attached to you."

Ashley nodded. "Okay."

"Because the worst thing in the world is when someone strings you along, when they're not really interested in dating you, but they pretend to be. And you fall really hard for them, and then suddenly they're just, like, not there any more." I stared out at the streetlight, my eyes blurry with tears.

I knew Mary-Kate was talking about my situation, and she was right. I had to talk to Ben, and tell him that even though I liked him a lot, I just wanted to be friends – nothing more.

But I also knew that Mary-Kate was talking about herself. And even though she was trying to hide it by making jokes, she was still really hurt. I could see her trying not to cry, too.

I'd heard more than enough. I couldn't stand seeing Mary-Kate so unhappy for so many days in a row just because Jake wouldn't listen to her apology or explanation. He wasn't acting like a nice guy. He was acting like a jerk. And if he wouldn't listen to Mary-Kate, then he was going to have to listen to me!

chapter eleven

If Mary-Kate knew what I was doing, she'd probably kill me, I thought.

It was first thing Monday morning, and I was searching the halls for Jake's locker. My plan was to talk to him about Mary-Kate. *I don't know what I'm going to say,* I thought nervously. *But I'll come up with something.*

I hate confronting people. I almost never do it – I avoid arguments whenever I can. But there was a lot on the line here – namely Mary-Kate's happiness! I didn't want her to look back on turning sixteen and remember how Jake hurt her. She deserved better than that.

There he was – closing his locker and about to walk down the hall, away from me. I hurried up to him, glad that he was alone and not with a bunch of his basketball buddies.

"Jake, can I talk to you for a second?" I asked as I caught up with him. "It's really important."

His eyes widened when he saw me, but then he smiled. "Oh. Hi, Ashley."

"Hi. I'm . . . well . . . I wanted to . . ." I stammered. *Spit it out, Ashley!* I thought.

"Look, Jake. Do you or do you not like my sister?" I asked.

Jake stopped walking and stared down at me, his face registering confusion. I had sort of blurted out what I wanted to know – but there was no other way to get to the point. I was always teasing Mary-Kate about being too blunt, but maybe it wasn't such a bad thing.

"What are you talking about?" Jake asked. "Why are you asking me that?"

We stepped out of the way of the crowds in the hallway and into an empty classroom.

"Mary-Kate feels terrible," I said. "I mean, she has felt nothing *but* terrible ever since the day you found out from Ben that he was invited to our sweet sixteen."

"Yeah. Well," Jake said.

"Look – I know it's all messed up, but I also know Mary-Kate still really likes you," I said. "Here's what happened, and some of it's my fault, and some is Mary-Kate's, and . . ."

Focus! I told myself. *Stop rambling!*

"First of all," I said, "we did plan on having an

all-girl party at first. But then Mary-Kate wanted to invite you, so she did, and she was sure she could convince me to change the party to include boys. But I said no," I explained. "I still wanted it to be a girls-only party. That's why Mary-Kate uninvited you."

"Okay . . . " Jake said slowly.

"But, at the same time, I met Ben. And I really liked him, and wanted to invite *him* to the party. So I did, because I decided that we should invite guys. I got home and told Mary-Kate that the party should include boys, after all. But before she got the chance to tell you about it in person, you heard from Ben that he was invited and you never heard Mary-Kate's side of the story!" I finally stopped to take a breath. Jake was standing there with a stunned expression. He might have heard enough, but I wasn't done yet.

"You really hurt her because you won't listen to her," I said. "She's been totally honest with you, and you won't even give her a chance."

Jake shifted from one foot to the other. "Okay. What can I say? I'm sorry."

"Thanks. But I'm not the one you should be apologising to," I said. "You should be talking to Mary-Kate." I started to walk away, but then I turned around. "I don't think you're a bad guy. It's just . . . Mary-Kate's my sister."

The bell rang, and I rushed out of the

classroom, eager to get away from Jake. I couldn't believe I had just laced into him like that!

I hope it works, I thought. *I hope I didn't just make things worse for Mary-Kate!*

"So, ready for your final spin before the big test?" Ben asked.

I had just walked out of school on Monday afternoon, and I was totally surprised to see Ben standing outside. He didn't even go to our school! "What are you doing here?" I asked with a laugh.

"I figured we should go to our lesson together," Ben said. "I mean, this *is* a special occasion when you think about it."

"It is?" I said.

Ben nodded. "This is the last time we'll ever see Ms. Junger again! Our life's going to be so empty without her telling us to check our mirrors."

"Yeah, I don't know how I'll handle it," I joked as we fell into step beside each other.

Mary-Kate's words from our conversation the night before suddenly came back to me. *If you really think you don't like Ben that way you should tell him. And you should tell him soon, before he gets more attached to you.*

I looked over at Ben. Should I tell him now? But that would be awkward – we were going to drivers' ed together. We'd have to sit in the same car for an hour.

But there wasn't going to be a good time. And if I didn't tell him soon, we'd end up going to my sweet sixteen together, and then he might get even more attached to me. . . .

I sighed. Why had it been so easy for me to be honest with Jake earlier? And why was it impossible for me to be up front with Ben now?

"Since this is our last lesson, I thought we'd practise some specific skills for the test," Ms. Junger said as Janine, Ben and I stood outside Columbus High School on Monday afternoon. She glanced my way. "Ashley, why don't you go first?"

Because I don't want to? I thought as I got behind the wheel. *Because I'm completely afraid of taking the test*?

"Now, don't be nervous," Ms. Junger instructed.

Easy for her to say! I thought.

"Just remember everything you've already learned."

"Right," I said as I adjusted the rearview mirror.

Ben was sitting in the back seat. I caught his reflection in the mirror, and he gave me a big smile. That made me feel better. "Okay, so where are we going?" I asked Ms. Junger.

She glared at me. "Nowhere, unless you put on your seat belt!"

"Oh – whoops. Sorry. I never forget that," I said as I quickly clicked the buckle.

"I guess you can't say *never* any more," Ms. Junger stated. "If you make that mistake during your test, you'll fail without even driving away from the Motor Vehicle Department!"

"I know, I know," I said quickly. "Sorry!" I always put on my seat belt whenever I got into *any* car. So why did I have to forget now? Was it just the mention of the test that had me flustered?

"All right. We're ready. Please pull out and take us over to Hanover Street," Ms. Junger said. "You remember, we've practised driving there before."

I nodded and turned the key in the ignition. Hanover Street was a very quiet street, so it was a good place to work on turns. I checked to make sure no cars were coming, and pulled out on to the street. I waited at the stop sign, then took a left. I glanced over at Ms. Junger to see how I was doing.

"Keep your eyes on the road at all times!" she commanded.

"I am, I am!" I insisted.

"Really, Ashley. Have I taught you nothing?" Ms. Junger complained.

"Actually, you've taught us all a *lot*," Ben piped up from the back seat. "I'm sure Ashley's just off to a slow start today, that's all."

"Hmm," Ms. Junger grunted.

"And, hey, slow starts are good. I mean, you taught us all not to jam on the gas pedal, right?" Ben joked.

Ms. Junger let out a little snort that sounded slightly like a laugh.

I was really grateful for Ben coming to my rescue. He could even make Ms. Junger laugh, which was amazing. *I really do like him,* I thought. *He's a great guy. Maybe I won't break up with him – at least, not just yet.*

I started to relax as we pulled on to Hanover, and I practised my three-point turn. Now, if only Ben could be in the back seat when I had to take the test!

"Ashley! The curb!" Ms. Junger suddenly warned me.

I braked just as the wheels tapped the curb. "Sorry," I said.

"Don't apologise," Ms. Junger coached me. "Just relax and do it again. You're a good driver, Ashley. You can do it."

I felt grateful that she wasn't yelling, but no matter what she said, I couldn't relax. My hands clutched the wheel as I started another turn.

I couldn't help feeling that I wasn't ready for the test – or my party – or turning sixteen at all!

chapter twelve

The big day had finally arrived. Wednesday afternoon. My driving test.

You can do it, Ashley, I chanted to myself all the way to the Motor Vehicle Department. *You can do it, you can do it, you can do it . . .*

I was so nervous I hardly remembered getting into the driver's seat. But somehow I must have buckled my seat belt, checked my mirrors, started the car, and driven off with a motor vehicle officer sitting next to me.

"Okay, Ashley. Take the next right turn available," he instructed.

My hands were a little sweaty as I gripped the wheel more tightly. So far, I seemed to be doing okay. I hadn't made any major mistakes, anyway. Ms. Junger had told us the tests would take only about five to ten minutes, so I couldn't have too much left to do.

"Now pull over under that big tree," the officer told me. "And complete a three-point turn."

I gulped. This was one of the parts of the test that I hated – but that was why I'd practised it endlessly yesterday afternoon with Mom and Dad!

Remember, Ashley – it's all just angles, I told myself as I turned the wheel to the left. I backed up carefully, without hitting the curb. Then I turned the wheel again and completed the turn.

"Nice job," the officer said. "Now proceed out on to the street to the lights and take a left."

Ms. Junger's words came back to me. "Just relax. You're a good driver, Ashley. You can do it." When we turned back into the motor vehicle office lot, the officer told me to park right in front.

I carefully put the car in Park and turned off the engine. There was a moment of silence while the officer completed some paperwork. It felt like the longest two minutes of my entire life!

"Congratulations, Ashley. You passed!" the officer finally said. He handed me a sheet of paper.

"Yes!" I cheered. "Thank you, thank you, thank you!" I gave the officer a big hug. His face turned bright red. "Ummm, you can take this inside and we'll finish up now – or we can go ahead with your sister's test and complete the process when you're both done."

"Thanks! I'll wait," I said as I unclipped my seat belt. When I got out of the car, Mary-Kate and Mom were waiting for me. "I passed!" I said in a whisper.

Mary-Kate gave me a quick hug. "That's so awesome!"

"Your turn. Good luck!" I told her. "And remember, if I can do it, you can do it."

I stared at the paper in my hand. I couldn't believe it! I actually had my driver's licence!

I was almost done with my driving test. I felt good behind the wheel – confident. Seeing Ashley pass the test had definitely helped.

I had done everything right so far, or at least I thought I had. I'd obeyed all the street signs correctly. I'd parked on a hill. I'd backed up in a straight line and done a three-point turn.

"Okay, please turn right here, into the parking lot," the officer said as he made a check mark on his clipboard.

Check marks are good, I thought. That had to mean that I was doing things right!

I turned into the Motor Vehicle Department lot. I was done! I had passed!

"We need to park this at the back, so please go past that Jeep," the officer said.

"Okay." I glanced over at the Jeep. It was red – just like Jake's Jeep! I looked more closely.

Wait a second – it *was* Jake's Jeep!

The door opened and Jake climbed out. *What is he doing here?* I wondered, glancing at him in the rearview mirror.

"Watch it!" the officer said as I ploughed into an orange pylon cone set up for a motorcycle test.

"Sorry!" I said, jerking the wheel to the left. I ran over another cone, and slammed on the brakes. There was a loud screech.

The officer cleared his throat. "Okay, that'll be enough."

"I'm sorry!" I said. "I just got distracted. See, I know that guy, so – I'm really sorry, I don't drive like that usually and—"

The officer shook his head. "I'm sorry. This test is over. If you'd please just pull over there and park, we'll go inside and we can talk about a retest." He made some more notes on his clipboard.

"Retest?" I yelped.

"I'm sorry," the officer said as I quietly parked the car. "But you failed the test."

My heart sank as I got out of the car. "Well?" Ashley asked, jogging over to me.

I shook my head.

"What? You didn't pass?" she asked.

"No. Didn't you see how I took out those cones?" I asked. "It was awful."

"Maybe so. But your day is taking a turn for the better," Ashley said. She pointed to the left.

I turned and saw Jake walking towards us. My stomach jolted. I strained to see if he was smiling or frowning. Was he glad to see me?

"What are you doing here?" I asked him.

He's smiling, I realised now that he stood in front of me.

"Mary-Kate, you wrote it in my day-planner in capitals," Jake said. "Four o'clock – Mary-Kate and Ashley get their licences. And I think there's a 'Yahoo' on there, too." He glanced at Ashley and smiled.

My stomach was full of butterflies. It was the old Jake, the *nice* Jake. What was going on?

"I know you probably have to get going, but could you come sit down with me for a second?" Jake asked.

"Um . . ." I glanced over at Ashley, who for some reason looked like she knew more than she was letting on.

"I have to go in and do all the paperwork," Ashley said. "Mom and I will meet you inside."

"Yes, don't forget – you'll need to come in, too," the officer said to me. "To schedule another test."

"Okay – I'll be there in two minutes," I promised.

"Another test?" Jake asked.

I grimaced. "I failed. Can you believe it?"

"Well, I did see the way you mowed down

86

those cones!" Jake laughed. "It was kind of ugly."

"It's all your fault. I was passing until I spotted you!" I said.

"Sorry. But you know what? I failed my driving test the first time, too," Jake said with a grin.

"Really? No way! You're such a good driver."

"*Now* I am. But on that day? Forget it. I was so hyper that I made about five mistakes." Jake led me to a bench outside the brick building. "Just reschedule the test. You'll do fine next time."

We sat down. "I'll try to be quick, so I don't hold you up too long."

He turned to me and put his hand over mine. "I'm really sorry for the way I've been acting."

I bit my lip, waiting for him to go on.

"The reason I was so mad is that I thought you came up with the all-girl party idea as an excuse not to invite me," Jake said. "I thought you didn't want me there."

I nearly fell off the bench. "What? But why wouldn't I?"

"I don't know! It's the only thing that made sense to me," Jake said. "But someone explained that I was wrong."

Really? I thought.

"It was just a huge mix-up all along," Jake said. "You were trying to change the party because you wanted me to be there – not the other way around."

"That's what I tried to tell you," I said. "But you wouldn't listen!"

Jake nodded. "I know."

"It really hurt my feelings that you didn't believe me," I confessed. "Why would I lie about something like that? Why would I lie to you at all? I wouldn't."

"I know – I mean, I realise that now," Jake said. "And I'm sorry." He squeezed my hand. "Do you think you could maybe think about, you know, getting back together?"

I was dying to get back together with him. But after all he'd put me through, I figured he could sweat a little.

"I'll think about it," I said.

"Oh." He stared down at our hands. A look of sadness spread across his face. "For how long?"

"Umm . . . about five seconds," I replied. "Yes, Jake. I would like to get back together with you."

"Really?" Jake asked.

I nodded.

Jake leaned closer and kissed me. I kissed him back, my heart leaping with excitement. A few people walking into the motor vehicle office stopped and glanced over at us, but I didn't care. Finally, I was back together with Jake!

"Wow," I said, scooting closer to Jake. "What made you come here today to tell me all this?"

"Well, I talked to Ashley yesterday. Actually,

she talked – I listened," Jake said. "You know, I think it's been more than two minutes. We'd better go inside."

We went into the building. While Jake went over to Mom and Ashley, .I checked in with the clerk at the desk and told him I wanted to reschedule. Ashley was standing behind the little blue line and smiling for her picture. I was so jealous! I'd even take a *horrible* photo on my licence, as long as I *got* one.

"Let's see. The next possible date is" – the clerk checked his computer – "June thirteenth."

June 13! Our birthday – and the day of the party!

I stared at him. "No way. Aren't there any other openings?"

He shook his head. "Nope. Not until the middle of July."

The middle of July? That was eons away!

"Okay, I'll take it," I said. I glanced over my shoulder at Jake, who was talking with Ashley and Mom. If Jake could pass the test on his second try, then so could I.

Besides, now that we were back together, I felt like anything was possible – even finding the perfect place for our sweet sixteen in the next – gulp! – eight days!

chapter thirteen

An hour after passing my driving test, I was cruising down the highway with the radio on and a smile on my face. Mom let me drive us home in the Volvo. Right now she was on her mobile with Dad. She had called to give him the good – and not so good – news about our tests.

There was nothing like the feeling of being behind the wheel and knowing exactly what I was doing. Why had I worried so much about the drivers' test? I passed with flying colours. I couldn't believe Mary-Kate hadn't.

I glanced in the rearview mirror. Mary-Kate was sitting in the back seat, gazing out of the window with a sort of dreamy smile on her face. She didn't seem to care much about the test now that she was back with Jake. I looked at the road ahead of me. I realised that I'd missed seeing

Mary-Kate so happy. I was just glad I'd had a tiny bit to do with it.

"Excuse me – Ashley?" Mom said. "I don't mean to criticise, but, um—"

"What? Am I going too fast?" I quickly checked the speedometer. "No, I'm going thirty – that's the speed limit."

"It's not that," Mom said.

"Did I miss a sign? Am I swerving?" I asked.

"Honey, all I wanted to ask is – where *are* we? I wasn't paying attention to where we were going, because I was talking to your father. But I don't recognise this area at all." Mom peered out the front window.

"Mom, this is Oceanside Drive," I said. "We take this road almost every day."

"Yes, but we don't live in this direction. You're going south. We need to go north."

"Oh." So maybe driving *and* navigating was a bit too much for me on my first day as an official driver. "Oops."

"Why don't you pull over at the next scenic viewpoint, and we'll turn around there," Mom suggested with a wry smile. "I promise not to get distracted by any more phone calls."

"How did I do that? I mean, I've been on this road a hundred thousand times," I complained.

"Well, it's not like any of us was paying attention. You were too busy having fun driving, I was talking, and Mary-Kate . . ." Mom glanced over the back of her seat. She turned back to me. "I don't think she's with us, if you know what I mean."

"She's on Planet Jake," I said knowingly.

A few minutes later, I spotted a sign, and signalled before turning into it. I pulled into the small parking lot and made a slow, gentle curve to point us in the opposite direction.

"Wait!" Mary-Kate suddenly yelled. "Stop the car!"

I slammed on the brakes, thinking I was about to run into something. "What now?" I asked.

"What is it – a dog? A cat?" Mom looked frantically around the small parking lot.

"No. It's that *house*!" Mary-Kate cried.

I tried to follow Mary-Kate's finger, to see where she was pointing, but I had a bad angle. The house was behind us, to the right, perched on a rocky cliff over the ocean.

"Why don't you pull over and park," Mom suggested to me. "We can get out and stretch our legs and check out the place."

I had barely put the car in Park when Mary-Kate flung her door open and raced towards the large white house. "There's a sign out front, Ashley – come on!"

I didn't realise what she was so excited about until I followed her to the house. Then I saw it: the sign. FOR RENT : AVAILABLE FOR PHOTO SHOOTS AND

Special Occasions. Call for Information.

"Wouldn't this be the perfect place for our party?" Mary-Kate asked me. "It's big enough. It's very glamorous. And it's on the beach, practically, with a gorgeous view, like we promised in our invitations!"

"You're right," I said as we wandered around the front lawn. "This place would be awesome for our party."

"I agree," Mom said.

"You do?" I asked.

She nodded. "The house is beautiful, and the setting is perfect. Imagine the photos you could get. Besides that, all of your guests would be very impressed."

"Then can I borrow your phone to call Wilson and see what he thinks?" Mary-Kate asked excitedly.

"Sure – hold on, and I'll get it for you," Mom offered. She jogged over to the car, which gave me and Mary-Kate another minute to stand and admire the house. It was the best location we'd seen, by far. I hoped it wouldn't be out of our price range. *And* I hoped it would be available eight days from now!

"Here you go." Mom handed her phone to me. "Wilson's number is programmed."

I dialled, then Mary-Kate leaned against my shoulder, and we both pressed an ear to the phone. We waited a few seconds for the call to go through. After it rang twice, Wilson answered. "Hello, Olsens!" he said cheerfully. "Was I supposed to call you today? I knew something slipped my mind – I'm sorry. I'm down here in the Bahamas. So what's up?"

"Wilson, we're calling because we're standing outside the place where we've decided to have our party!" Mary-Kate announced.

"Pizza Pals?"

"No!" Mary-Kate and I both said at once.

Wilson laughed. "Okay, then where are you?"

"We're standing on Oceanside Drive. We just passed the most gorgeous house – it's perched on the cliffs above the ocean," I said. "There's a sign here saying that the house can be rented!"

"Hmm. It sounds wonderful. I think I may know that house," Wilson said. "Is there an address on it?"

"Let's see . . ." We walked closer to the house so I could read the number by the door. "It says 14375 Oceanside."

"Sounds familiar. What's the phone number listed? I'll cross-check it in my database," Wilson said.

I read off the phone number from the sign. A few seconds later, Wilson sighed. "Sorry, guys. It's not available. The owner allows only certain kinds of events there, and I know for a fact her policy is not to rent it out for any kids' events – ever."

"But we're not *kids*," Mary-Kate protested. "We're almost sixteen."

"*I* know that, but I tried to rent it before, and she said nobody under twenty-one," Wilson said. "I'm so sorry, guys. You're right, it *would* be an awesome location. Oh, no – I've got to run, but I'll call you later – we'll get this location thing solved! I promise."

I turned to Mary-Kate as I clicked off the phone. "Well, so much for that idea."

"Wait a minute. If she'll rent only to people twenty-one and over . . ." Mary-Kate tapped her chin as she stepped back to look at the house. She glanced over at Mom, who was sitting on the car's bumper. "Then we'll just have to be twenty-one."

"Do I look twenty-one?" I asked Ashley as I walked into her bedroom right before dinner. I twirled around in my faded jeans, hooded sweatshirt and untied sneakers. "I figured we should call the owner of that house right away to let her know we're interested."

"Good idea," Ashley agreed. "You don't look twenty-one, but maybe you can sound twenty-one." She handed me the slip of paper with the house address and the owner's phone number on it. I quickly dialled, anxious to get this over with. If she said yes, great. If she said no, we needed to get back to Plan B – or rather, Plan Pizza Pals. I shuddered at the thought.

"Hello, McKenzie Real Estate Holdings. This is Bridget McKenzie," a cheerful voice answered.

"Hi," I said. "I'm calling because my sister and I are interested in renting a house we saw – and this number was listed on the sign, 14375 Oceanside?"

"Yes, that's one of our properties."

"Oh, *good*. Well, we were wondering if the building would be available next Thursday – June thirteenth," I said.

"What would you be using it for?" she asked.

"It's our birthday party," I said. At least that much was true. "We're turning twenty-one, and we've been looking for the perfect place to have a big party. We already have the music and the caterer lined up – and our parents would be there, too."

Ashley shook her head. "Don't talk about our parents!" she whispered. "That makes us sound too young."

I shrugged. "Too late," I mouthed.

"Let's see. I just need a little more information," the woman said. "Did you want the house for the entire day?"

"Late afternoon and evening," I said.

"Okay. Well, you're in luck. It looks as though the house isn't booked for that day."

"Great!" I exclaimed.

"However, I like to meet all of the renters in person before I let them use the space. So if you don't mind, could you and your sister meet me at the building tomorrow afternoon? Say, three o'clock?"

Pretending to be twenty-one over the phone was one thing. But convincing someone in person . . .

I bit my lip, wondering if we could pull it off. Then I realised that if we didn't go after this, we'd be stuck at Pizza Pals for sure.

"Yes. Three o'clock would be perfect," I told her. "Thank you so much!" A minute later, I hung up the phone with a smile. "Done!"

"Are you kidding?" Ashley cried. "You mean we have the place?"

"Yup," I replied. "There's just one little thing we have to do first."

"It's so awesome that we both got our driver's licences. I told you that you'd do fine, didn't I?" Ben and I took a seat at a black wire table at the ice cream shop later that evening.

"Yeah, but I didn't believe you," I said.

"You just needed to focus. Which was probably a lot easier to do without me in the car to distract you, right?" Ben joked.

"Right. That must have been it." I smiled.

Come on, Ashley, I thought. *If you can confront Jake Impenna in the middle of a school hallway, you can do this.*

"Ben, I have to tell you something," I began. I was so nervous that my hand was shaking, so I set my dish of ice cream on the table. "And it's kind of hard for me to say, so I hope I don't mess it up or hurt your feelings."

"I know what you're going to say," Ben said. "You really miss our driving lessons."

I smiled. "Not exactly."

"You don't really like mint chocolate chip, right? It's okay, you can tell me. I can take it," Ben joked.

Why was he being so funny and cute? It was making this *so* hard. "Actually, it's about us," I said, looking down at the table. "I was thinking that maybe we should . . . be . . . just friends."

Ben didn't say anything for a minute, and I finally got the nerve to look up at him. He was actually almost smiling. "Yeah. You know, I was thinking the same thing."

"*What?* You were?" I asked. Here I was, agonising over breaking the news to him – and it turned out that this wasn't news at all?

"Ashley, I think you're great – you're so nice, and pretty, and fun to be around. But, um . . ."

"No sparks?" I guessed.

He nodded. "No sparks. Which is a good

thing, because those can really cause eye injuries."

I laughed. "So weren't you ever going to say anything?"

"Sure. I just didn't want to say it before your sweet sixteen party. I know it means a lot to you. And if you were counting on me to be your date, I didn't want to let you down." Ben licked his ice cream cone.

I sat there and took a bite of my sundae. I couldn't help feeling momentarily stunned. Here I'd been afraid to tell Ben I didn't like him as a boyfriend. And he'd been worried about telling me that he didn't want *me* as a girlfriend! So it was true, we really weren't a good match.

Even though I knew it was stupid, I couldn't help feeling a little insulted. Shouldn't Ben be heartbroken about our break-up?

Then again, he was still cool, and good-looking and funny. There wasn't anything wrong with *him*. We just didn't click the way a boyfriend and girlfriend are supposed to. I was glad we'd both decided to be honest with each other. There was just one thing, though . . .

"Ben? I still really like you – as a friend. So if it's okay with you, would you still come to our sweet sixteen, as my sort-of date?"

"Are you kidding?" Ben asked.

I held my breath. Had I said the wrong thing?

Then he grinned. "I would not miss that party for the world. Your e-mails have everyone totally intrigued. But you know, Ashley, you can tell *me*. Where's it going to be? What's this mystery location?"

"You'll just have to wait and see," I said.

And so will I, I thought. It was either a gorgeous mansion by the ocean . . . or a kids' restaurant with a dinosaur out front!

Tomorrow is the day, I thought. Tomorrow we'll find out if we're having the party of our dreams, or a Pizza Pals nightmare!

chapter fourteen

"I *still* can't believe you agreed to do this!" I said to Mary-Kate. I tried not to wobble in my high-heeled pumps as I walked up the sidewalk to the giant white house on Thursday afternoon. I was wearing one of Mom's dresses, stockings and pumps. Mary-Kate was wearing a blazer and black pants. She'd actually told Bridget McKenzie we'd be coming from work! We'd done everything we could think of to look older than we were.

"This is *it*, Ashley," Mary-Kate said as we walked up the steps to the porch. "If we can't get this settled today, we have to call Pizza Pals and confirm our reservation for the Pals Party Room. If that doesn't motivate you, I don't know what will."

"Don't worry, I'm motivated," I said. I knocked on the front door of the house, and a tall woman with long red hair immediately came to open it.

"Hello," she said. "Are you here to discuss the rental?"

"Yes, I am," I said. "I'm Ashley Olsen, and this is Mary-Kate. You must be Ms. McKenzie?"

"Please, call me Bridget." She narrowed her eyes at us for a second. "Come in!" Bridget stepped back to let us into the house.

"Thank you." I walked in and nearly gasped as I glimpsed the house's interior. Three picture windows side by side gave a perfect romantic view of the ocean. There were separate living rooms where people could hang out and talk, and a big open floor space with a high ceiling that would make a perfect dance floor.

Bridget gestured for us to take a seat on the sofa in the largest room. I noticed Bridget examining me carefully.

"So, we're desperately hoping we can rent this gorgeous house for our birthday party," I began. "We drove past this house the other day and it just took my breath away. When we saw your sign, naturally we were thrilled."

"Yes. Most people are," Bridget said. "This house has been in my family for quite some time, so as you can imagine, I'm very protective of it. Very," she insisted.

"Oh, I understand, completely," I agreed.

"So. You mentioned your birthday party. And

you two girls are going to be . . . how old?" Bridget asked.

"Twenty-one?" Mary-Kate said, sounding unsure of herself.

I cleared my throat. "Twenty-one," I said with a little more force.

"Really. That's exciting," Bridget said with a polite smile.

"Oh, yeah. Twenty-one. We're hitting the big time," Mary-Kate said. "Getting old. Moving away from home."

"You still live at home?" Bridget asked.

"Y-yes," I stammered. Why did I feel like were we saying all the wrong things?

"I thought you'd be off on your own by now – didn't you say something about coming here from work?" Bridget asked.

"Uh, yes," Mary-Kate answered. "Summer jobs. Internships, really."

"Oh," Bridget said. "So you're in college?"

"College. Of course," Mary-Kate said. "We're there all the time. Constantly. We – we love college."

"We just live at home to, ah, save money," I added. "Classes and books and all. Very pricey."

"Right. That can add up." Bridget leaned back and looked from me to Mary-Kate and back again. "Do you girls go to the same college?"

"Yes," I said.

"Which one?" Bridget asked.

"UCLA," Mary-Kate said.

"USC," I said at the same time.

Bridget raised an eyebrow. I thought I saw a slight smile play across her lips. I laughed nervously.

"Well, see, we take some classes at UCLA, and some at USC," Mary-Kate added.

Bridget smiled. "So, what are the two of you majoring in?"

"Uh," I mumbled.

"We're majoring in, um, science," Mary-Kate said.

"Science. That's kind of vague, isn't it?" Bridget said. "Which science, exactly?"

I was sitting there racking my brain for an answer: Biology? Chemistry? Astrology? Engineering? What sounded right? What sounded grown-up?

Suddenly I couldn't take it any more. Mary-Kate and I didn't lie like this. I felt really awful about trying to pull this off.

I blinked back the tears that were welling up in my eyes. "I'm sorry," I said, getting to my feet. "I can't do this, Mary-Kate."

Mary-Kate hung her head. "I know . . . neither can I."

"Girls, what's going on here?" Bridget asked.

"Ms. McKenzie, we've wasted your time. None of this is true. We don't go to college. We just really, really wanted to have our sweet sixteen party in this house," I explained.

"So we came here pretending to be twenty-one. But we're really not," Mary-Kate finished for me.

"We didn't want to lie, but we just – well, we're desperate." I tried to muffle a sob, but it didn't help. A tear slid down my cheek.

I rummaged through my bag for a tissue, and blew my nose. "I don't know why I'm telling you this. None of it is your problem." I sniffled. "We'll go now – sorry."

Mary-Kate sighed. "I'm sorry, too. This was really stupid of us. Thanks for meeting with us anyway." She put her arm around me. "It's okay, Ashley," she whispered.

Together, we headed for the door. I couldn't get out of there fast enough. We crossed the porch and sat down on the front steps.

A few more fat, warm tears spilled down my face. "Pizza Pals won't be that bad," I said, trying to convince myself as much as Mary-Kate. "Wilson can put some kind of beach mural on the wall – and we can play a CD of ocean sounds until the DJ starts – right?"

"Right," Mary-Kate agreed. "And we have a really good DJ, so, you know, it'll be fine."

"Yeah," I sighed. "Just . . . fine."

The door opened behind us. Bridget stepped on to the porch. "Girls, come on inside and let's talk. I think I may be able to help you after all."

I stared up at her. "Really?"

"You're kidding, right?" Mary-Kate said.

She smiled. "No, I'm not kidding."

A million thoughts raced through my mind as we walked back into the house. Was Bridget really going to let us use the place? Why? What had changed her mind?

"First, I should tell you that it wasn't cool that you lied to me. But, at the same time, I admire your guts," Bridget said with a smile. "You girls have a lot of ambition. And if you tell me just a little bit more about your party, and what it'll be like, maybe I'll give you my approval."

I nodded, sat up straight, and cleared my throat. "Okay. First, we want to apologise again for trying to fool you. We're really, really sorry." Then I quickly described the party – who was coming, and how our parents would be there to chaperone.

"We promise, it's going to be a *fun* party – but not a wild, out-of-control party," Mary-Kate added. "We're going to have dinner, dancing – with a DJ – and a big birthday cake… and that's it."

"What do you mean, that's it?" Bridget laughed. "Sounds pretty fun to me."

"Maybe you'd like to come?" I offered.

Bridget smiled. "Maybe. I'll have to check my schedule. Now, here's a list of our daily rates for renting the house." She handed a brochure to

Mary-Kate. Mary-Kate's eyes widened as she skimmed the brochure. *Uh-oh*, I thought.

My heart sank as Mary-Kate said, "I'm not sure we can afford this. We have a budget, and we just can't go over it—"

"Hmmm . . . well, we do have special rates for USC students." Bridget winked at us. "What if we cut the rate to . . . a hundred dollars flat."

"Really?" I asked.

Bridget shrugged. "Sure."

"No way. You normally get thousands of dollars for this place. You're being *too* nice," Mary-Kate said, looking guilty. "We don't deserve this."

"Let's just say I have my own reasons for helping you girls out. I mean, I was your age not that long ago," Bridget said. "I know how important it is to have big events work out the way you want them to. If you didn't have the party here, where were you going to have it?"

"Pizza Pals. You know that kids' restaurant on Highway Twelve where they have rollerskating waiters and clowns?" I said.

Bridget started to laugh. "Do you think I could let that happen? You know, this is a very funny coincidence. When it was time for my high-school graduation party? My parents decided they would plan the entire thing. I kept trying to tell them what I wanted, but no. They rented out a pizza parlour, and hired a cheesy magician." She shuddered. "Do you have any idea how long it took to live *that* down?"

I giggled. "I'm so sorry. That's awful."

"Tell me about it," Bridget said. "So, I think we're all set here. You can get in touch with your caterers. They'll want to know where to bring the food, and they may need to speak to me about arrangements. Which caterers are you using?"

"Menu by Margo," Mary-Kate said.

"Oh! Perfect. You won't be disappointed," Bridget said. "She's been here before, so she knows the set-up. I'm going to get myself a glass of water – would you girls like some?"

"Thanks, that would be great," I said. "Can I help?"

"Oh, no – I'll get it," Bridget said. "You just call Margo and I'll be right back."

"Wow, she is *so* nice. This is working out perfectly," Mary-Kate said once Bridget had left the room. "Ashley, how did we ever pull this off?"

"All it took was hard work, dedication, and about a ton of luck," I admitted.

"Now there are only two things left to stress about," Mary-Kate said. "My driving test. And the actual day of the party!"

chapter fifteen

"What colour should we pick?" I asked Mary-Kate. We were standing by the wedge-shaped nail polish display at Salon 21 on our birthday. There had to be a hundred colours to choose from!

"Here's the question. What looks perfect for our birthday *and* matches our dresses *and* will show up nicely in pictures?" Mary-Kate's eyes sparkled with excitement as she studied the different colours.

I knew how she felt. This was the most thrilling day of our lives – so far, anyway. It was hard to focus on nail polish!

"If I were you," Mom said, "I'd go with something that picks up your dress. Which would be . . ." Her fingers skimmed the top of several bottles, searching for the right shade. "Ah-ha! Here it is." She lifted a bottle of a rich royal blue-black with sparkly silver flecks mixed into it. "Night Magic."

"I love it," I said. "What about you, Mary-Kate?"

"The little sparkles in it will catch the light," Mary-Kate observed as she held up the bottle. "Let's do it. Thanks, Mom!" Then she handed the bottle to the manicurist who was politely waiting for us.

"Night Magic it is," she said. "Everyone can use a little magic, right?"

"You go first," Mary-Kate said to me.

"Actually we can take both of you at once," the manicurist said. She gestured to another table, where a different manicurist was waiting.

"Thanks – that's great!" I put my hand over my mouth as I yawned. "Sorry, I was so excited about today that I couldn't sleep last night," I told the manicurist as I sat down.

"Neither could I," Mary-Kate said, sitting at the next table along. "I kept worrying about taking my driving test, and if the DJ will play the songs we requested, and if everyone who says they're coming will actually show up, and if they'll like the party, and if it'll rain—"

"What? It almost never rains here." I laughed. "And you almost never worry that much!"

"What can I say? Turning sixteen has changed me dramatically," Mary-Kate joked.

"Yeah, right," I said as the manicurist rubbed lotion into my hands. "Sure it has."

Being pampered like this wasn't something that happened very often – I was totally loving it.

First Mom and Dad had woken us up by bringing us breakfast in bed – complete with fresh strawberries and whipped cream, Dad's famous French toast, and cappuccinos. They'd both taken the day off from work to spend with us, and we'd all gone for a walk on the beach together.

When we got home, we had at least ten birthday voice-mail messages waiting for us, from Brittany, Lauren, Jake, Ben and some of our other friends. The day was perfect so far. And it could only get better!

"You know what? While you're doing this, I'll go get you two something to drink," Mom said. "I'll be back in twenty minutes or so, okay?"

"That's so nice," I told her. "Thanks!"

"Any idea what your mom's giving you for your birthdays?" the manicurist working on Mary-Kate's nails asked us.

Mary-Kate glanced over at me, and we both shrugged. "*No* idea," we said at the same time.

"Whatever it is, they're saving it for our party tonight," I said. Unless the gift *was* our party, as they kept insisting!

"What do you think, Mary-Kate? Will this work for you?" Sonja, the hairstylist, swiveled my chair and held a mirror up behind my head to show me her work.

My eyes lit up as I saw the detailed weaving of

my hair into a smooth, sophisticated style. In the front, a few tendrils of my long blonde hair curled as they fell against my cheeks. After our manicures, we'd had our make-up done by the beauty artist at the salon. I hardly recognised myself in the mirror. I mean, I couldn't remember the last time I looked so put together. And we didn't even have our killer dresses, accessories, and shoes on yet!

"It looks incredible – you're amazing!" I told Sonja. "How did you do that?" I glanced over at Ashley, who was sitting next to me and having her hair styled by Ruben, the salon owner.

"Ashley, what do you think?" I swirled around in my chair to show her the complete look.

"Wow!" she said.

"Nice work, Sonja," Ruben said with admiration. "One of your best. Tell you what – when we both finish, let's take a picture of Mary-Kate and Ashley for our book."

"Your book?" I asked as Sonja unclipped the cape around my shoulders and brushed a few stray hairs off my collar.

"We keep a photo book of our clients," Ruben explained. "So we can show off our best work. Not that we had *that* much to do with it. You girls are naturally beautiful."

I got out of the chair and shook out my arms to stretch a bit. "Did you *see* me when I walked into this place? I hardly slept last night and I looked like a zombie."

"But a zombie with potential," Ashley joked, smiling at me.

"Right. We'd love to be in your book!" I said. "So when Ashley's done, you can take our picture . . ." I glanced at the clock to see how we were doing on time. I gulped. "Uh-oh. Ashley, my driving test is in an hour!"

"Then you'd better get going," Ashley said.

"Wait a minute – you did all this for a driving test?" Ruben joked.

"It's a long story," I said. I hurried over to Mom, who was reading a book in the waiting area. "Mom, we have to get going to the Motor Vehicle Department."

"Sorry, I got completely caught up in this story!" She got to her feet and studied me for a moment. "Mary-Kate, you look beautiful! More beautiful than usual, that is."

I laughed. "Do you think I could come here every week?"

We quickly stopped to say goodbye to Ashley. I wouldn't see her until we met at the house just before the party. "Good luck on your test – I know you can do it, Mary-Kate," she said.

"Thanks." I grabbed my bag. "Come on, Mom."

"Don't worry, honey – Dad will be here to pick

you up, cover the bill, and take you home to change," Mom told Ashley.

I leaned over and squeezed her hand. "See you later! And don't worry, I'll be there on time. Thanks, everyone!" I called over my shoulder as we dashed out of the door.

Two minutes later, Mom and I were completely stuck in traffic. We weren't moving at all. We'd never make it to the test, and have time to get home for me to change into my dress!

"Mom, if we take this next exit and drive on the back roads instead, won't that take us right past our house?" I asked. I stared out of the window at the endless line of cars and trucks ahead of us.

"Well, I suppose, yes," she said.

"And if we did that, couldn't I run in and get dressed and *then* go to the driving test?" I asked.

"Hmm. I don't know." She glanced at the clock on the Volvo's dashboard. "It's about ten minutes to our house if we jump off here."

"And we could get to the motor vehicle place on the back roads, too, which wouldn't have this major traffic jam," I reasoned.

"Sounds like a plan to me. Except – can you get dressed in ten minutes?"

"Mom, for this, I can get dressed in *five*," I said.

Of course, I might have my shoes on the

wrong feet, I thought. But I could always fix that later!

I slid into the driver's seat and clipped the seat belt around me, careful not to wrinkle the fabric of my dress.

Then I reached up to check the rearview and side mirrors. I wasn't making any mistakes today – not one!

"You're a little more formally dressed than you were last time," the motor vehicle officer said, giving me a curious look.

"Yes. I have a big party right after this, and it's my birthday," I said. I hoped he didn't think I'd dressed up just for the test!

"Well, happy birthday," he said in a formal tone. "Now let's proceed with the test."

I nodded and waited for his instructions. When I started the engine, I realised driving in heels wasn't going to be the same as driving in my usual shoes. But no problem – I could handle it.

I checked over my shoulder before pulling out of the parking space. A curled strand of hair fell in my face and blocked my vision.

"Oh, come on," I groaned. I blew the hair away from my eyes and pulled on to the street.

I squirmed in my seat a bit to make myself more comfortable.

"Ouch!" I yelped. My skin was stuck to the vinyl seat because of my backless dress.

"Everything okay?" the motor vehicle officer asked.

"Fine! Just fine!" I insisted. I pushed the stinging sensation out of my mind. Nothing would stop me from passing this test today!

Suddenly another car pulled into traffic from a side street, right in front of us! I backed off the accelerator and slowed down, avoiding the car.

"Nicely done," the officer said. "You reacted very well."

I heaved a sigh of relief as we proceeded to the traffic light. I waited until we had the green Turn arrow, then drove on to the quiet street we'd used before, as instructed.

I slowly made my three-point turn, being careful not to step on my long skirt as I worked the pedals. As I turned around from backing up, I caught a glimpse of my hair in the rearview mirror. So far I hadn't made any mistakes, and I hadn't ruined my hair.

So far, so good!

"You're doing much better today," the officer said as we returned to the parking lot at the Motor Vehicle Department.

Don't blow it now! I told myself. *Don't even look at any other cars – or any other people, not even Mom!* I slowly pulled into the spot, put the car in Park, and shut off the motor. I glanced nervously at the officer's clipboard, holding my breath.

He looked up at me. "Congratulations, Mary-Kate. You passed!"

The best thing about taking your driving test just moments before your sweet sixteen party is that you're pretty much guaranteed to take a great photo for your licence.

"Okay!" the official photographer said. "Smile!" He snapped the picture. I raced around to his monitor to check how I looked.

I sighed. Perfect. Absolutely perfect.

The photographer chuckled. "We'll send you your photo licence in about two months. You know, it's a little fancier than most people's pictures, but for you, it works."

I grinned. "Well, I was worried I wouldn't look good so I thought, you know, I'd dress up."

He laughed. "Really? Just for this?"

"No, I have a big party to go to," I admitted. "So, am I done?"

"You're done here," he said.

"Great! Thanks a lot!" I called as I ran outside to meet Mom. "All finished," I told her. "You know what? It was much easier the second time around. So, shall we head to the party?" I held my arm out, expecting Mom to take it. She had changed at the house during our brief pit stop and was all dressed for the big event.

"I'm sorry, Mary-Kate. I can't drive you to the party," Mom said.

I stared at her and felt all the colour drain out of my face. "But, Mom! Why? I have to get there – Ashley's going to freak out. We have to leave – now."

Mom shook her head. "No, *I* have to leave now. I have a last-minute errand to run."

I protested. "But—"

"And besides, that nice-looking boy over there said he could give you a lift." Mom pointed across the parking lot.

I turned and spotted Jake striding towards us. He was wearing black chino pants, a blue button-down shirt, and a patterned tie. I'd never seen him so dressed up before. He looked so handsome, it took my breath away. I couldn't think of what to say.

Fortunately, that didn't last *too* long. "I did it, I did it!" I called as I ran towards him.

He wrapped his arms around my waist and lifted me into the air. I squealed with happiness. "All right," Jake cried. "You passed! And happy birthday!"

"Thank you!" He set me down and I hugged him tightly. "Thanks for encouraging me to take the test again!"

"You're welcome. Now, come on, Mary-Kate," he whispered in my ear. "We have a party to get to." He took my hand and slipped his car keys into my palm.

"Really?" I asked. "You're going to let me drive?"

"Of course. It's your birthday, isn't it?" He put his arm around my waist as we walked towards his car. So far this was the most awesome birthday ever – and the party hadn't even started yet!

chapter sixteen

When I walked up to the party with Jake, Ashley was standing on the front porch, looking at her watch.

"What took you so long?" she asked. "I was starting to worry you wouldn't get here in time."

"Sorry – I was busy passing my driving test," I replied.

"You passed?" Ashley asked. "Awesome!" She gave me a high-five.

I stepped inside the house and glanced around. "Ashley, this place looks amazing!"

"I know!" Ashley said excitedly. "And everyone's starting to arrive."

"Can you believe our sweet sixteen is actually here? About to happen?" I asked.

"I can," Jake said. "She talked about it the entire way over." He smiled at me. "Hey, I think I'll go inside and see if there's anything your parents want me to do. You guys will be okay, right?"

I nodded. "Thanks for letting me drive!" Once Jake was inside, I grabbed Ashley's hand. "Can you believe this day? Can it get any better?"

"I think it's about to," Mary-Kate said as the DJ started to play some music.

"Can you see – is everyone here?" I asked Mary-Kate as she peered down at the first floor from the top of the stairs.

"I hope so," she said. "I don't think many more people can fit in the door!"

"Oh my gosh – I can smell the food cooking. It's the fajitas. Mary-Kate, my stomach is growling – can't we go downstairs yet?" I asked.

"How can you think about eating? My stomach's doing nervous flips," Mary-Kate said. "Do you think everyone's going to have a good time? Do I look okay?"

"You look great," I said. "How about me?"

"Perfect," Mary-Kate said. Then she turned to look down the stairway again. "Mom and Dad are talking to the DJ!"

A few seconds later, the music stopped. I held my breath. Now I had butterflies in my stomach, too. This was it. Our big introduction!

"Whatever you do, please, please, please do not let me trip down the stairs," I said to Mary-Kate.

"Here – take my hand," Mary-Kate said.

"Hello, everyone, and on behalf of Mr. and Mrs. Olsen, I'd like to welcome you to Mary-Kate and Ashley's sweet sixteen," the DJ said into the microphone. "Without further ado, I'd like to introduce the birthday girls – the girls everyone is here to celebrate . . . may I present Ashley Olsen and Mary-Kate Olsen!"

He clicked on one of our favourite dance songs as Mary-Kate and I walked down the stairs together. Everyone was cheering and applauding and yelling as we descended the staircase. I was so happy I didn't know whether to laugh or cry!

"Isn't this incredible?" I said to Mary-Kate, almost yelling to be heard above the crowd and the music.

"This place is packed!" she said. "And it's all for us."

"We could never have pulled this off if we didn't work together," I told her. "Thanks for being the best sister in the world – and my best friend!"

We hugged each other at the bottom of the stairs, then headed straight for the dance floor.

Our sweet sixteen was just the way I'd always imagined it – only better!

"Having fun?" Jake asked as I put my hands on his shoulders. The DJ was playing the first slow song of the evening, and Jake and I were dancing together.

"I think I can say without exaggerating that this is the best night of my entire life," I told him. "And it's partly because of you."

"Well, thanks. But I think your family gets *most* of the credit!" Jake said.

"I know," I said, blushing. "I'm just really glad you're here to share this with me."

"So am I. And if I haven't said this before, you look incredible tonight." He brushed my cheek with his fingers.

"You've said it a few times, but a few more times would be okay, too," I said. "Thanks."

When the song ended, Jake and I headed over to the refreshment station to get some punch. When I turned around, I saw Dad standing at the microphone instead of the DJ.

"Attention, everyone. Could I please have your attention? We'd like to give Mary-Kate and Ashley their birthday presents now," Dad announced. "If they wouldn't mind coming up here?"

Ashley and I walked forward, and Mom reached into a bag and took out two envelopes. She handed one to each of us.

I reached into the envelope and pulled out a very official-looking piece of paper, from the U.S. Treasury. "What's this?"

"A savings bond?" Ashley said. She looked up at Mom and Dad and smiled. "Gee, thanks. This is great."

"Yeah, thanks!" I added. It was sort of a boring present, but I didn't care – not when our party was so great.

"You know what?" Dad shook his head. "This is stupid, but I left the paperwork that goes with your savings bonds out in the car. Would you two mind going outside to get it? Should be right on the passenger seat, or in the glove box."

"Uh, okay," I said.

"Savings bonds, huh?" Ashley mumbled as we headed outside. "I guess that's why we never found anything in our present hunt. I mean, they're pretty thin – easy to hide—"

"Ashley, look!" I cried. There, in the parking lot, in the closest spot – where Dad's car *had* been parked when I showed up – was a vintage pink Ford Mustang convertible. There was a huge red bow on the hood, with a poster-sized card that said *Happy Sweet 16, Ashley and Mary-Kate*!

"*What*? Is that for *us*?" Ashley squealed. Together, we started to race over to the Mustang.

"Of course it's for you!" Mom said.

I turned around and realised Mom and Dad had come outside behind us – and so had every single guest at the party!

All our friends were crowded on to the porch and the front steps.

"Like we'd really get you some boring old savings bonds for your sweet sixteen," Dad said.

He tossed me a set of keys. "Happy birthday!"

Everyone started to cheer and clap as Ashley and I opened the Mustang's doors and jumped into the car. "This is so awesome!" I said. "Can you imagine us driving around town in this? No wonder we couldn't find our present in the house!"

"We'll take turns driving," Ashley said. "Where do you want to go first?"

I leaned on the horn and waved to the party crowd. "Thanks, Mom and Dad!" We jumped out of the car and ran over to hug our parents. "This is the most generous gift ever. Thank you so much!" I said as I hugged Mom.

"Thanks, Dad – how did you know we wanted a Mustang?" Ashley said.

"Doesn't everyone?" Dad joked. "But there's something else. Only we need to talk to you about it in private, if that's okay."

I glanced at Ashley. This sounded even more intriguing than the car. "Sure thing. You guys go back inside and get dancing – we'll be there in a second to cut the birthday cake, okay!" I called to everyone.

"Don't take too long!" Brittany yelled.

"We want cake, we want cake!" a couple of guys chanted as everyone drifted back into the house.

"What was so important that you needed to

talk to us in private?" Ashley asked as we perched on the front steps.

"You know the big summer music festival I've been organising," Dad said. "With some of your favourite bands."

I nodded eagerly. "Of course."

"Well, you're sixteen now. And that means you can try new things, take on new adventures," Mom said.

"Right . . ." Ashley glanced at me to see if I knew where this was headed.

"I've arranged jobs for both of you this summer," Dad finally said. "Working at the music festival!"

"*What?*" Ashley and I both screamed.

"It's not as glamorous as it sounds," Dad said. "You'll be working very, very hard – with long hours doing set-up, and selling T-shirts and things like that. But you'll be paid, and when you're finished with whatever work you're doing, you'll get to see the bands perform. And hanging out day after day around the bands means you'll meet some of the musicians."

"Dad, thank you so much – working at the festival sounds incredible!" Ashley said.

"You guys are way too generous. You've given us this great party, plus the car, plus got us these jobs . . ." I looked at both my parents and smiled. "This has been the most amazing party, the best night of our life – and now this summer's going to be even *more* exciting!"

Ashley looked at me and smiled. "I can't wait to hit the road!"

Find out what happens next in

Sweet 16

Book 3:

THE PERFECT SUMMER

"Oooh! We are so going to be late!" I said as I glanced away from the road to check the clock.

"Can you please stop being Miss Responsible for one second and appreciate the tremendousness of this moment?" Mary-Kate said, tipping her head back to look up at the clear blue sky. "We're in our own car, cruising up the coast, heading for the coolest summer ever!"

"I know! I know," I said with a grin. I gave myself a moment to savour the feel of my hair whipping around in the wind and the sun on my face. "I still can't believe that dad was able to score us jobs at the coolest music festival of the summer!"

Mary-Kate pushed her purple tinted sunglasses up on her head and grinned at me. "What do you think our assignments are going to be?"

"Maybe we'll get to be personal assistants to the stars," I said dreamily.

"Or maybe we'll get to work in wardrobe, picking out costumes for all the acts," Mary-Kate suggested. "Whatever we do, I'm sure we're going to get to hang with famous people."

"I know! And they're going to pay us to do it!" I added.

"What are you going to do with all the mad cash we're going to make this summer?" Mary-Kate asked.

"I am going to buy the Kentmore 2000

surround sound stereo with ten disc changer, dual cassette deck, and four remote speakers."

Mary-Kate laughed. "Wow. You've put a lot of thought into this already, huh?"

"I guess I have," I answered with a shrug. I gave her a sly look out of the corner of my eye. "You have no idea what you're going to buy, do you?"

"I have *some* ideas," Mary-Kate said, adjusting her sunglasses. "I'm thinking a whole new wardrobe, or maybe a DVD player for my room, or maybe I'll get something for Jake . . ."

Mary-Kate trailed off and looked out of her side of the car with a little sigh. I could tell she missed her boyfriend already and I wondered what that was like. Aside from my parents and my friends, I didn't have anyone special to miss this summer.

"Omigosh! Ashley!" Mary-Kate yelped suddenly.

"What?" I asked. "What is it?"

"I think you missed the turn-off!" Mary-Kate said. She grabbed the map and the directions up from her lap and studied them.

"Oh, no," I said, gripping the steering wheel harder. "What do I do, Mary-Kate?"

My sister groaned. "I can't believe this is happening. Our first road trip together – and we're totally lost!"

mary-kateandashley

Meet Chloe and Riley Carlson.

So much to do...

so little time

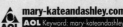

mary-kateandashley

TWO of a kind ™

Coming soon – can you collect them all?

HarperCollins*Entertainment*

 mary-kateandashley.com
AOL Keyword: mary-kateandashley

  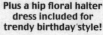

From Books for Real Girls

It's What YOU Read

b the 1st 2 kno
mary-kateandashley

REGISTER 4 THE HARPERCOLLINS AND MK&ASH TEXT CLUB AND KEEP UP2 D8 WITH THE L8EST MK&ASH BOOK NEWS AND MORE.

SIMPLY TEXT SS, FOLLOWED BY YOUR GENDER (M/F), DATE OF BIRTH (DD/MM/YY) AND POSTCODE TO: 07786277301.

SO, IF YOU ARE A GIRL BORN ON THE 12TH MARCH 1986 AND LIVE IN THE POSTCODE DISTRICT RG19 YOUR MESSAGE WOULD LOOK LIKE THIS: SSF120386RG19.

IF YOU ARE UNDER 14 YEARS WE WILL NEED YOUR PARENTS' OR GUARDIANS' PERMISSION FOR US TO CONTACT YOU. PLEASE ADD THE LETTER 'G' TO THE END OF YOUR MESSAGE TO SHOW YOU HAVE YOUR PARENTS' CONSENT. LIKE THIS: SSF120386RG19G.

HarperCollins*Entertainment*

PARACHUTE PRESS

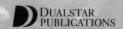

DUALSTAR PUBLICATIONS

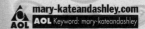

mary-kateandashley.com
AOL Keyword: mary-kateandashley

TM & © 2002 Dualstar Entertainment Group, L.L.C.

Order Form

To order direct from the publishers, just make a list of the titles you want and fill in the form below:

Name ....

Address ....

....

....

Send to: Dept 6, HarperCollins Publishers Ltd, Westerhill Road, Bishopbriggs, Glasgow G64 2QT.

Please enclose a cheque or postal order to the value of the cover price, plus:

UK & BFPO: Add £1.00 for the first book, and 25p per copy for each additional book ordered.

Overseas and Eire: Add £2.95 service charge. Books will be sent by surface mail but quotes for airmail despatch will be given on request.

A 24-hour telephone ordering service is available to holders of Visa, MasterCard, Amex or Switch cards on 0141- 772 2281.

Collins
An *Imprint* of HarperCollins*Publishers*